"What are you doing, Annie?" Chase said harshly. "What are you doing to me?"

"Nothing, Chase," she murmured. "Nothing."

But it just wasn't true. She was doing plenty. Her lips were parted, just asking to be kissed. Her body was pressed against his. Everything about her was breathless and soft.

"Maybe we shouldn't," she said, her breath bathing him as she spoke.

"No maybe about it," Chase agreed. But he closed his hand in her hair and gently drew her head back even further, exposing the white skin of her neck and a delicate heartbeat at its base. "We shouldn't," he said, settling his mouth on hers again, a full kiss this time. "Should not," he whispered, drawing away yet staying close.

Without thinking, he slid his hand to the small of her back and felt her arch in response. She averted her eyes, but a tiny sound emerged, a sound that made him kiss her again. He was breathing hard when he broke away. "We shouldn't even get near each other."

She nodded, breathless. "Which one of us is going to stop?" she asked.

"I'll stop," he said, gathering her up in his arms, hugging her close in a surge of male energy. "Leave it to me." Blood steamed through his veins as he kissed her again. He cupped her face, his eyes stormy in his need, tender as he saw the concern in hers.

"I am going to stop, Annie," he said, making an effort to gentle his voice. "But not until we've had as much pleasure as we can stand. . . ."

WHAT ARE *LOVESWEPT* ROMANCES?

They are stories of true romance and touching emotion. We believe those two very important ingredients are constants in our highly sensual and very believable stories in the *LOVESWEPT* line. Our goal is to give you, the reader, stories of consistently high quality that may sometimes make you laugh, sometimes make you cry, but are always fresh and creative and contain many delightful surprises within their pages.

Most romance fans read an enormous number of books. Those they truly love, they keep. Others may be traded with friends and soon forgotten. We hope that each *LOVESWEPT* romance will be a treasure—a "keeper." We will always try to publish

LOVE STORIES YOU'LL NEVER FORGET
BY AUTHORS YOU'LL ALWAYS REMEMBER

The Editors

Loveswept ® 541

Suzanne Forster
Child Bride

BANTAM BOOKS
NEW YORK · TORONTO · LONDON · SYDNEY · AUCKLAND

CHILD BRIDE

A Bantam Book / May 1992

If you would be interested in receiving protective vinyl
covers for your Loveswept books, please write to this address
for information:

Loveswept
Bantam Books
P.O. Box 985
Hicksville, NY 11802

ISBN 0-553-44215-5

Published simultaneously in the United States and Canada

PRINTED IN THE UNITED STATES OF AMERICA

OPM   0 9 8 7 6 5 4 3 2 1

For Leslie, Tara, Kerry, and Bob—
my quality assurance team.
Thank you!

One

The whining snap of a rawhide whip scorched the silence and sent a flock of turkey buzzards laboring toward the desert sky.

The sudden crackling sound brought Annie Wells to a complete stop. Dust swirled, coating her ragged tennis shoes as she turned to scan the rocky trail she'd just traveled, searching for the source of the noise. It had sounded like the unforgiving lash of a bullwhip. How many men could there be who used such a whip as a weapon? *Only one whom she knew of.* Sweat trickled down her forehead and into her eyes, stinging them. Her senses sharpened almost to the point of pain as she watched and listened.

All she could see for miles was bone-white Wyoming badlands, cobalt sky, and the golden powder stirred up by the buzzards' flight. All she could hear was the crack of the whip ricocheting eerily off the canyon walls.

Annie waited, hardly daring to breathe, until the landscape grew still again. She'd been walking for miles, ever since the Greyhound bus let her off in Painted Pony, the closest town to the foothills where she was headed. The punishing journey had seemed endless, but now the parched, quivering air held a promise of something about to happen. She could feel it, the way an animal senses a disturbance in the elements. And then, somewhere in the near distance, she heard a dog barking and a horse nickering softly.

Annie's heart lurched crazily as she turned toward the sounds. The horse whinnied again, its plaintive report coming from behind a nearby ridge. Barely aware of her bruised shins or the burning fatigue in her calf muscles, she hurried toward the outcropping of rocks and spindly piñon trees. As she reached the embankment, she dropped to her knees. What she saw in the shallow gulch below brought a soft gasp of recognition to her lips.

A man stood on the edge of a dry creek bed, his back to her, his shoulders wide against the blue and white horizon. He was a prodigiously tall man, with dark hair curling from the back of his sweat-ringed Stetson. His long duster coat, which nearly touched the ground, was the kind gunslingers once wore to conceal their sawed-off shotguns. But instead of a gun, this man held a huge bullwhip, coiled and ready at his side.

Annie ducked down, inhaling arid heat and dust as she peered over the rocks that hid her from view. She knew the man. She'd seen him in action before, with his bullwhip.

A rattling hiss pulled Annie's attention away from the man and riveted it on the deadly adversary he faced. Some ten feet to the man's right an enormous diamondback rattler held an excited Border collie at bay. Ready to strike, the swaying snake warned away all comers with its gleaming fangs and ominous death rattle.

The collie yelped, trembling, dancing.

The snake struck out, a flash of light and sinew.

Annie watched in mute horror as the man's bullwhip cracked the dry air like black lightning. It caught the rattler by its outstretched body, lifted it right off the ground, and hurled it into the creosote at the foot of the ridge where Annie was crouched. She muffled a cry as the huge reptile began to slither up the hill toward her. Reacting instinctively, she

scrambled to her feet, stumbling through loose limestone and spurs of sagebrush in her frantic rush to
get away.

She heard the man shouting at her not to move,
but he might as well have told her not to breathe.
She looked back, searching for the snake, and saw it
flashing away from her, a river of silver in the sand.
Relief poured through her like water, leaving her
dizzy and off-balance. As she fought to get her
footing, the rocks crumbled beneath her, giving way.

There was no chance to save herself, no chance
even to scream. She pitched forward onto all fours
and tumbled down the incline, end over end. Covered with dust and sage, her ginger-colored hair
flying from its restraints, she came to an unceremo-
nious landing virtually at the man's booted feet.

"Are you Charles Beaudine?" she whispered a
moment later, staring up into his blue-black eyes.
His face was as lean and hard and savagely beautiful
as she remembered. Nothing had changed, not the
burnished muscular contours, the squared-off jaw,
or the taut, sensual mouth. Even his dark brows
were still stormy enough to cast shadows.

"Maybe," he said. "Who the hell are you?"

Annie drew in a painful breath, trying to fill her
empty lungs. "I'm your wife."

"Take the hill, Smoke," Chase Beaudine told his
horse, flicking the reins as he urged the Appaloosa
gelding up a steep, boulder-studded side trail. The
shortcut, a rugged ride that climbed through a stand
of quaking aspens, would shave at least a half hour
off the trip to his cabin. Every now and then he
wondered at the wisdom of having isolated himself
so effectively in the foothills of the Wind River Mountains. And then he reminded himself why it had been
necessary.

The woman slumped against his chest moaned
softly, her head rolling into the curve of his shoulder
as the Appaloosa climbed upward, expertly negoti-

ating the steep rise. Crazy female must be sun-struck, Chase thought, feeling a stirring of sympathy as he clamped his arm tighter around her middle to better brace her against his body. She'd fainted dead away on him after mumbling that nonsense about being his wife.

She'd been in and out of consciousness ever since, but never long enough to answer his questions, and she carried no purse or identification. He couldn't imagine where she'd come from, unless she'd walked all the way from Painted Pony, which was a couple hours away by car. But who in her right mind would try a thing like that in the midafternoon heat?

"My wife?" His husky words of disbelief lifted strands of the woman's pale red hair. The closest he'd ever come to anything resembling marriage was his adolescent fixation on a tightrope walker when he'd been stationed at El Toro Marine Base. He'd parked his skinny eighteen-year-old butt on the wooden bleachers every chance he got, entranced by her high-wire work, and then he'd visited her trailer afterward, equally entranced by her versatility at lower altitudes. But even that had only lasted until the circus left town. Not that Chase had anything against matrimony. Weddings were fine. It was living together afterward that caused the trouble.

The Appaloosa surged upward, loose rocks flying in his wake as he snorted and lunged toward the crest of the hill. Chase dug his knees into the animal's girth for balance and grasped the woman tightly as her body jolted against his. Though mercifully quick, the trip to the top was a bone-jarring, teeth-rattling ordeal, and it took all of Chase's concentration to keep both of them aboard the powerful horse.

It wasn't until they'd reached level ground a short time later, and were cantering down an overgrown deer path, that Chase realized his palm was cupping something soft and full, something suspiciously pliant.

"What the hell?" he murmured. If that fullness was

what he thought it was, he was getting fresh with his passenger's upper anatomy. His first impulse was to release her immediately. His second was less gentlemanly. He worked his fingers cautiously and felt the warm, buttery flesh give way, melting beneath his palm. A bullet of pleasure shot straight for Chase's groin. He'd never felt anything so sweet and soft in his life. She was built small on top, but still sinfully curvy, as if she'd been sized perfectly for a man's hand.

Speaking of which—get your hands off her, cowboy.

The thought flashed through Chase's mind, but still he didn't act on it. Not right away. The slow rock of his horse's stride and the sighing warmth of the woman in his arms were stirring up some dangerous urges. A clutch of excitement took hold of him like warm, questing fingers, and the deep, tugging urgency of it went to work on his mind as well as his body.

He'd been a long time between women, and his imagination seemed determined to make up for lost opportunities. It was telling him what a rare pleasure it would be to lay her down in the sweet green grass alongside the trail and wake her up with the heat that was building between his legs. The scenario played out in his thoughts with the kind of detail that could give a man wildly erotic dreams.

In the fertile reaches of his imagination, he could feel her cool breath on his face and the heat rising off her slumberous body. He could hear the irresistible sounds of a woman aroused . . . the throaty little moans as he stroked the silk of her inner thighs. He could even imagine watching her eyes drift open as he came up against her woman's softness with that hard, aching part of himself. . . .

A low murmur brought Chase out of his daydream. She nuzzled into his arm like a kitten seeking a warm place to curl up. His hand was still molded to her breast, and the desire to do more than touch her burned through him like a short fuse attached to a big stick of dynamite.

The woman is out cold, Romeo. Stomp that fuse. Now.

By the time they reached the clearing where his small cabin sat up against granite bluffs, Chase had pretty well doused the last sparks kindled by his sexual daydreaming. His Border collie, Shadow, danced and barked eagerly as Chase dismounted and then lifted the woman off the horse and into his arms. She was light as a willow branch and painfully thin, he realized, cradling her gingerly as he carried her up the creaky wooden porch steps and into the house. Without knowing how he knew it, he had the disturbing awareness that she'd been through some incredible hell in her life.

Chase deposited her on a quilt-covered cot in the front room and, remembering the holster strapped to his thigh, freed the rawhide ties and laid the sawed-off shotgun on a wooden table next to the cot. Without bothering to remove his hat or his coat, he pulled up one of the log cabin's few pieces of furniture, a cane rocker, and settled himself into it.

In a situation like this a man needed some thinking time.

He rested a booted foot on his knee, sinking down in the chair until the back of the rocker caught his Stetson and tilted it forward. His dust-covered cowboy boot was about eye level, and without thinking twice, Chase used the boot's silver tip as a gunsight, zeroing in on the woman's dirt-smudged face and windblown hair. Who was she? he wondered, trying to recall if he knew her from somewhere. Or if he'd ever seen her before. She didn't ring any bells. Certainly not wedding bells.

He smiled faintly, not quite sure what it was about the woman that amused him. She was a tiny little thing. Plain, too, if what he could see of her features under the sweat and trail grime was any indication. Nope, his unexpected houseguest wasn't likely to win any beauty contests. And yet there was something undeniably appealing about her flyaway hair and her slightly off-kilter features. Her nose had a little bend at the bridge, and her full mouth was set tautly, even in repose, as though she hadn't yet completed her quest, whatever it was.

"What do you suppose she wants with us, Shadow?" Chase murmured as the collie wandered over, presenting his neck to be scratched. As Chase obliged the dog, he had a sudden, disturbing thought. She could be another reporter looking for the inside story on "Chase Beaudine, reluctant hero." It wouldn't be the first time one of those tabloid sharks had tried to flush him out. But none of them had gone to this much trouble, he reminded himself, smiling at the irony of a rag reporter risking sunstroke and rattlesnakes for the sake of a story.

Chase was contemplating the woman's ragged jeans and her torn cardigan sweater when she stirred and croaked out a word he could barely hear.

"What is it?" he asked, sitting forward.

"Water—"

"Yeah, sure thing." Peeling his long, rangy frame out of the low chair, Chase headed across the room to the kitchen sink and pulled a glass from an unfinished pine cabinet. He hadn't bought the three-room cabin with gracious living in mind. He'd just wanted a place to escape to at the time, and he hadn't seen the need for anything beyond the basics—a bedroom, a bathroom and a living room and kitchen. Not a place a woman could get excited about, he imagined.

He filled the glass to the brim with crystal-clear mountain-spring water, returned to the cot, and sat alongside her.

"Say when," he said, holding the glass to her lips as she attempted to lift her head. Chase saw immediately that she needed help, and he slipped his hand into the silky hair at her nape, propping her up so she could drink. For reasons he couldn't begin to fathom, he found it incredibly sexy to have a vulnerable woman sipping from one of his glasses, taking the cool, sweet spring water he offered.

Good God, he thought, he was going to need a cold

shower if he kept this up. Next he'd be having erotic fantasies about soothing her fevered brow and taking her temperature.

She nodded when she'd had her fill. "Thank you," she said, gazing up at him with eyes so unflinchingly blue, they made him want to grab an extra breath. As she rested her head on the pillow, a rivulet of water made a tiny trail through the dirt on her chin.

Chase nodded, wondering why in the hell he couldn't think of what to ask her first. Who *was* this perplexing woman? Where had she come from? He had a couple other very pertinent questions he needed to ask her. But instead he heard himself saying, "Want me to clean some of that dirt off your face?"

"Yes, please."

Yes, please, Chase thought. She had a sweet way of putting that. He pulled the red handkerchief from around his neck, dipped the end of it into the glass of water, and began carefully to wipe the grime from her face. After a moment of his gentle strokes she closed her eyes, and even that innocent response sent a strange laser of desire through him.

Please, God, he thought, as he worked his way down toward the shell-pink fullness of her lips, don't let her open her mouth until I'm done. Not even to talk. It didn't seem right for a plain little thing like her to have such a sensual mouth.

His wrist brushed against her faded pink cardigan sweater as he worked, drawing his attention to its severe lines and old-fashioned collar. The sweater was buttoned fastidiously all the way to the top, and it looked tight enough at the neckline to cut off her oxygen. No wonder she'd fainted.

"Can you breathe okay?" he asked, feeling foolish as he lifted the edge of her collar. "Would you like me to loosen this up?"

"Yes . . ." She said the word softly, and without opening her eyes. "I would like that."

Chase set the water glass down on the table and drew in a protracted breath as he began to work free the buttons of her sweater. He had three of them undone and was wondering how much farther he ought to go when she opened her eyes and looked up at him. She seemed to be taking him in, noticing things for the first time.

"Do you always wear your hat and coat in the house?" she asked.

Somehow it wasn't the question he'd expected. And neither was the inquisitive expression that animated her features. The corner of his mouth twitched, more a bemused grimace than a smile as he started to shoulder out of the duster coat, then stopped himself. He was uncomfortably aware that he wasn't behaving like himself, and that she had him at a disadvantage in some inexplicable way. "Depends," he said, drawing the coat back on.

"Depends on what?"

"The weather indoors." He intended his brusque tone to discourage conversation on such a topic. But some women didn't know when to quit, Chase reminded himself as she blinked up at him, all blue eyes and curiosity. She looked as fragile as an abandoned child, and taking care of her forced a gentleness out of him that was alien—especially since his work demanded the gut instincts and lightning-quick reflexes of a hired gun. Even now the same ruthlessly competitive male drive that had always impelled him to take risks other men shrank from was telling him to quit playing wet nurse—and take control of the situation.

"Weather in here seems fine," she murmured.

"Am I imagining things, Missy, or are you pretty anxious to get my clothes off?"

She blushed slightly, but it was the graceful way her dark eyelashes swept up and her eyes turned to liquid that mystified and enchanted Chase. He could feel the pit of his stomach going soft and the area south of it going drum-taut.

Somewhere in the logic centers of his brain, an emotional traffic signal was flashing steadily. PROCEED WITH CAUTION, it was telling him. SHARP CURVES AND

SOFT SHOULDERS AHEAD. But Chase couldn't drag himself away from her shimmering gaze long enough to pay much attention to it. His heart was pounding, and his throat was as parched as the dry stream bed where he'd met her. Take control? He couldn't have found his own butt in an outhouse.

Enough of this, he told himself.

He bent over her, fumbling to redo the button he'd been working on, and then he rose abruptly and yanked off his hat. The Stetson sailed through the air like a Frisbee and landed on the kitchen table. The duster coat took wing and ended up in a heap on the floor next to the table.

"All right," he said, drawing in a breath as he turned back to her dangerous gaze. "I want to know what's going on here. Who are you?"

"Annie Wells," she said without hesitation.

The name didn't strike Chase as familiar, but the way she was looking at him, with such unwavering certainty in her expression, made him ask, "Am I supposed to know you, Annie Wells?"

"Yes. Most definitely. You married me five years ago."

"*Married* you? What kind of nonsense is that, woman?" Obviously she wasn't playing with a full deck. But the last part of her statement couldn't be dismissed quite so easily. Five years ago? "I wasn't even in this country five years ago," he said. "I was—"

"In Central America." She finished the sentence for him, then added in a voice that wavered slightly, "You were on a recovery mission for the Pentagon in Costa Brava, and I was one of the Americans you rescued."

Chase felt as though he'd been blindsided. Memory rocketed him back to a time and place he'd made a concerted effort to forget. The mission in Costa Brava had been a nightmare for him personally. He and his partners in the recovery operation, Johnny Starhawk and Geoff Dias, had been sent to the tiny Central American republic to liberate several American scientists trapped during a rebel insurrection. Once inside the country, they'd split up, trying to locate the Americans. The only survivor he had found was a teenage girl hiding in a bombed-out convent. Tragically he hadn't been able to get her out of the country alive. She'd been killed in a car accident on the way to the border. And he, too, had nearly been killed.

"You've got the wrong man," he said harshly, trying to shut off the disturbing wash of memories and the surge of mixed emotions accompanying them. Disbelief, anger, guilt, welled up in him. Who the hell was this woman?

"No, it was you—Charles Beaudine. The man who rescued me had your face, your eyes. He called himself Chase. He even used a bullwhip. Oh, *please,* you must remember! I was hiding in a convent near San Luis when you found me. I'd been there a month, ever since my parents were killed by guerrillas." Her voice cracked slightly, as if it was difficult for her to continue. "I remember every detail. You were wounded in a fight with one of the rebels. He had me in his rifle sights, and you took the gun out of his hands with your bullwhip. He pulled a knife, remember? He cut you."

Chase felt a spark of pain from the scar on his leg where the knife blade had caught him. His heart was thundering as he walked to the door and swung it open, breathing in hot, pine-sharpened summer air and struggling to make sense of the situation. There had to be a logical explanation, but try as he could to come up with something, only one answer made sense. Who, besides a muckraking reporter, would have any interest in bringing up the Costa Brava mission? And who else would know the details? She must have got her information from newspaper reports, sketchy as they were.

"Why won't you believe me?" she said, a hurt quality to her voice, "I'm telling the truth."

He turned back to look at her and saw that she'd lifted herself up with some effort and was resting her shoulder against the log wall of the cabin. Her eyes were expectant and fearful, but they were also suffused with another emotion that tugged at him. Desperation. She was pleading for something, but what was it? Recognition? What did she want from him? With a massive effort of will he hardened himself against the vulnerability that drenched her blue gaze like a summer shower.

"I'm telling the truth, too, Annie Wells. As sure as I'm standing here, I've never seen you before in my life."

She couldn't be who she said she was, Chase told himself. That girl was dead, God help her. Dead with her blood on *his* hands. He'd been the one driving when the jeep had gone off the embankment. He searched his memory for an image of the teenager, anything he could use to prove to himself that this women couldn't be her. But all he got were fuzzy shapes and outlines. The high fever and bouts of delirium he'd suffered during the mission had impaired his memory—and undoubtedly his judgment. The car wreck had finished the job, leaving him with nothing but occasional flashbacks that were too stark, yet fleeting, to understand.

He had told Annie Wells the truth, but not the whole truth. He couldn't remember the young woman whose life he'd saved, and then destroyed. He couldn't even remember her name.

"I'll prove it to you then," she said, almost defiantly. "Ask me anything, anything at all."

"I intend to ask you plenty," Chase assured her. He didn't make a habit of terrorizing vulnerable women, but he was going to get some honest answers, even if he had to put the fear of God into her. He'd been working for the Cattlemen's Association since he'd settled in Wyoming, and he'd flushed out plenty of cattle thieves and horse rustlers in that time, even put a couple of them away, in self-defense. He could sure as hell handle one tiny female.

"Keep talking," he said quietly, taking his shotgun

from its holster. He rubbed the barrel across the leg of his jeans as though the metal needed polishing. It was a casual move, even offhand, but the gun took on a presence all its own in that small, still room. "And make it a damn good story."

Annie Wells couldn't seem to breathe deeply enough to fill her lungs. She'd had some fearful premonitions about what might happen if and when she found Chase Beaudine, but never this. Never that he wouldn't believe her. He didn't even appear to remember her, which seemed impossible to her. How could he have forgotten what they'd been through together? The hell . . . the *heaven*. She would never be able to escape the memories, no matter how long she lived, or how far she traveled. Her only safe course now was to stick to the facts, to relate exactly what had happened.

"Your wound turned bad," she told him, severely curbing the emotion she felt. "Infections are deadly in a subtropical climate. You could have died of the fever alone, so I took you to a priest—"

"For what? Last rites?"

"This priest had been a *curandero*—a Spanish medicine man—before he converted. He knew how to use medicinal herbs and plants. He gave you an infusion of *arbuto* roots for the fever, and then he made an antibiotic salve out of jungle fungi and lichens for your wound. When you didn't respond, he lit candles and prayed to the saints."

"Nothing like a fallback plan," Chase said dryly.

"Don't be so quick to scoff. You're alive." She hesitated, fingering the collar of her sweater uneasily. "He offered to help me, too, since I had no papers and no way to prove I was an American citizen. As a priest, he had access to certain kinds of documentation."

"What kinds of documentation?"

She answered immediately, afraid if she hesitated she might never get the words out. "In this case, a *certificado matrimonio*—a marriage certificate," she said, watching his reaction. "With an American as my husband, I would automatically get citizenship. If we were stopped by the military—or even by the rebels—there was a far better chance they wouldn't detain me if I was your wife. Without the papers I had no identity, no country. They could have held me indefinitely—"

"My wife?" he echoed softly.

Annie took some hope from the thoughtful way he said the words. "Yes, the priest insisted we take the vows. In Costa Brava priests are authorized to perform civil ceremonies, and he wouldn't give us the papers without one.

"So you're saying that I married you?"

He was rubbing his thumb along the wooden butt of the gun, and Annie could tell he still didn't believe her. Or perhaps he actually didn't remember. He'd been ill, delirious. "I know it sounds crazy," she admitted. "But it was only a formality, a means to an end. We both understood that."

"Maybe you understood that, lady," he said, his voice going cold. "But as far as I'm concerned, it never happened. The only vow I ever took was at the age of eight, when my father and mother tried to kill each other with the broken whiskey bottles they'd just emptied. Damn shame they didn't."

His eyes cut into her like the shards of glass he spoke of. "That was the day I vowed to die unmarried," he added quietly. "So tell me, Annie Wells, why would I break that vow for you?"

From across the room, Shadow, the collie, made a pleading sound in his throat, as if he could sense his master's turmoil.

Annie shuddered involuntarily. She had no idea how to respond to what Chase had just told her. "I don't know why you did it," was all she could manage to get out. "Maybe you were grateful."

"Grateful for what?"

Her chest felt full and tight. She wanted to tell him it was because she was the one who had kept him from dying. It was she beside him when the fever spiked and sent him into convulsions; it was she holding him. How could he forget?

"The priest gave you the medicine," she said at last. "But someone had to be there, night and day, until the fever broke." She averted her eyes, knowing she couldn't go into the details of that ordeal now. She was too emotionally shaken to describe the things she'd had to do.

Fatigue overtook her then. She let her head fall back and closed her eyes. It was agony being in the same room with him again after so many years. His nearness was dragging her back to a time when her feelings for him were raw and sweet and powerful. She'd been in love with him once, the way only a terrified young girl can fall in love with a man who risks his own life to save hers. Perhaps it was hero worship, but it was achingly real to her then. And it had nearly destroyed her when she thought he'd left her behind, escaped to freedom and safety without her. Not knowing whether to love or hate him, she did the only thing she could do, wait . . . wait for him to come back for her.

Now, as she forced herself to open her eyes, look up at him, meet his wary gaze, she wondered how she could have been so tragically naive. He hadn't come back for her. He'd obviously never intended to. A wave of bitterness swept through her as she tried to push the painful memories out of her mind. If she'd been harboring some childish notion all these years that he shared her feelings, she could certainly see now that he didn't.

"What do you want from me?" he asked her. He swung the shotgun around and set the butt down on the floor, propping the barrel against the rocker.

"An honest answer." She probed his dark gaze, praying it didn't reflect the state of his soul. "Do you know who I am, Mr. Beaudine? Do you remember me at all?"

There was only one honest answer to that, but Chase didn't intend to reveal it. He was staggered at how much she knew about the mission, and until he learned exactly who she was and what she wanted, he wasn't going to feed her any more information.

He recalled waking up in an American hospital after the accident. His partners, Geoff and Johnny, had filled him in on the details of the mission, explaining that they'd found him in the demolished jeep at the bottom of a deep ravine. Trees and jungle undergrowth had kept the jeep from rolling into a turbulent river, but the girl had been thrown free in the fall. Her body was never recovered, but one of her shoes was found floating in the shallows.

That accident had haunted Chase, perhaps all the more so because he couldn't remember what caused it. But what haunted him now was the girl's story. She knew too much, things she couldn't possibly have learned from newspaper accounts.

The sound of breaking glass jerked Chase out of his reflections. When he glanced up, Annie Wells was tucked into herself and shaking violently. On the floor in front of her was the shattered water glass she'd just knocked off the table, apparently while trying to take a drink.

"Hey, easy does it," said Chase, distinctly uneasy at the prospect of dealing with a distraught woman. "It's just water. I'll get you some more."

He strode to the sink and pulled another glass from the cabinet, wondering how he was going to calm her down. As he twisted the water tap, his mind jolted him with a strange and mesmerizing image . . . a redheaded girl lying warm and soft against his body, pressing herself to him, whispering something unintelligible in his ear.

The wet glass nearly slipped through his fingers.

It could have been anyone, he told himself, any of the women he'd been with over the years. But his stomach muscles tightened. As he filled the glass, he felt the shock of cold steel pressing between his shoulder blades. A gun barrel.

"Don't move a muscle," Annie Wells warned, "or I'll blow your head off."

"What the hell are you doing?"

"I'm a desperate woman, Mr. Beaudine," she said, her voice ominously soft. "I've been searching for weeks, and I've traveled thousands of miles to find you. So you're going to hear me out. And when I'm done, you're going to give me what I want."

Two explosive clicks sounded as she cocked the pump-action shotgun. Chase set down the glass and raised his hands.

Two

"Okay, let's hear it," said Chase, carefully tempering his voice. There was a shell in the chamber of the twelve-gauge shotgun she'd jammed into his shoulder blade, and the last thing he wanted to do was rile a woman holding a loaded gun. "Just what is it you want?"

"My birthright," she said, her breath shaking slightly. "I have no way to prove I'm an American citizen. You're the only person I know who can help me."

The last thing Chase wanted to do at the moment was argue with her, but he didn't have a clue what she was talking about. He'd suspected she was sunstruck. Now he was sure of it.

"Why me?" he asked.

"Because I've got a piece of paper in my pocket that says you're my husband. I've got nothing else to prove who I am except that. And it's no good unless you say it is."

"Paper?" Chase tried to turn around, but the gun barrel dug a hole in his shoulder. "What piece of paper?"

"The certificate the priest gave us."

"The marriage certificate? It couldn't be valid. I was delirious, and you were just a kid."

"I was sixteen. Fourteen is the age of consent in

Costa Brava. The marriage was legal there, and that makes it legal here."

"Legal?" Chase was more aware than ever of the twelve-gauge at his back. She was giving new meaning to the term "shotgun wedding." "You're sure about that?" he said. And then he caught himself. He was talking as if he believed her story! A flash of something close to panic hit him as he considered the possibility that everything she'd been telling him was true. They'd told him the girl had been killed, that she couldn't have survived, but maybe they'd been wrong. At any rate the woman holding him at gunpoint had a problem. And her problem had become his problem.

"What about a birth certificate?" he asked, searching for any other solution than the one she'd come up with.

"I don't have one. Or a passport. I don't even have an I.D. card with my name on it."

"You were born, weren't you? There must be a record of it somewhere." Again Chase started to turn around. Again cold metal dug into his back. She was beginning to annoy him.

"I was born all right," she said, her voice oddly hushed, "in the wilds of Costa Brava, in an area so remote, the only access was by boat or airdrop. My parents worked with the *indígenas*, the local Indian tribes. They were medical missionaries, and I guess they weren't in the mood to trek across three hundred miles of jungle to register my birth with the consulate. Either that or my records got destroyed when terrorists bombed the consulate for the third time that year."

Anger suddenly stole through her softness. "How I became a woman without a country is beside the point, Mr. Beaudine. The fact is, I am one."

The information didn't entirely surprise Chase. He'd been told by his partners that the Pentagon hadn't been able to track down any information on the girl who'd died during the mission. The consulate in Costa Brava hadn't been able to determine her identity either, but Chase had assumed it was because he couldn't provide them with a name or a description.

"What about relatives?" he asked.

"My dad's folks were missionaries. Died of a tropical disease, both of them. We lost touch with my mom's parents. They retired, somewhere in the West Indies, I think. There's no one else that I know of. "So . . ." Her voice was expectant, almost breathy. "Are you going to help me? Or am I going to shoot you?"

Some choice, he thought. "You said you had proof, a certificate. I'd like a look at it." As the pressure of the gun barrel lightened, Chase heard rustling noises behind him.

"Turn around," she ordered. "Slowly. No tricks."

Chase left his hands in the air, and as he turned to face her, he was aware of two distinct impressions. First, he'd never been held at gunpoint by a woman before, and second, the experience wasn't entirely unpleasant. Especially when the woman at the other end of the barrel looked like an angel gone slightly berserk. He'd thought of Annie Wells as plain when he first saw her. Now her eyes were glittery with determination and her hair, catching the sunlight, was a flash fire.

The transformation was striking, and he had no way to explain it except for the desperation that must be driving her to take such crazy risks. She wasn't hedging her bets. She was going for broke, and as much as that must have frightened her, apparently it also excited her. She was sending up more sparks than a summer brushfire on a dark night.

"Here," she said, holding out the document for him to inspect as she wielded the shotgun with one hand. "Go ahead and read it, but stay there, right where you are."

The crumpled piece of paper Chase scanned was printed in Spanish and bore two signatures at the bottom. One of them stood out dramatically, a broad sprawl of loops and bars that was unmistakably his. He knew enough Spanish to verify that the form was what she said it was—a marriage certificate. Trouble, Beaudine, he thought. Big time.

"What do you plan to do now?" she asked.

For a fleeting second triumph sparkled in her alert gaze. It was gone almost before Chase caught it, but he recognized the implicit message. She had him, and she knew it. His neck muscles began to tingle, tensing ever so slightly. If there was one thing Chase Beaudine hated, it was being had.

"Probably not a whole lot while you're holding that gun on me," he said, letting his eyes slide up the barrel to where the wooden butt was cushioned against her shoulder. Her stance pulled the sweater tightly over her breasts, practically inviting him to check out curves that seemed indecently lush on so slender a frame. He flexed his hand with the memory of touching her there and felt an answering contraction deep in his gut. His thoughts steamed up immediately, and the heat must have shone in his eyes as he looked up at her.

"Did we consummate the union?" he asked.

She looked startled. "What?"

"Consummate. Did we do the deed? Did I get into your blue jeans, Annie?" He hesitated, his voice dropping lower, becoming huskier, as he stared into her widening eyes. "Did I get into you?"

Now she looked horrified. And then wildly unsure. "Yes," she said finally as heat flamed up her throat and reddened her pale face. It was pretty much the reaction Chase had expected. Annie Wells was a lousy liar.

"I guess it must have been pretty good," he observed, watching her reach protectively for the neckline of her sweater. Her fingers worried one of the buttons he'd undone. "Too bad I don't remember the details. Was it? Good?"

She nodded jerkily, still avoiding his eyes.

"Are you going to tell me about it?"

The gun slipped in her grip as she shook her head. "It's been too long. I don't think I can—"

Chase had her exactly where he wanted her—totally off guard. "Annie?" She looked up at him, and he caught her soft, frightened gaze, holding it suspended. "Don't mess with guns that are bigger than you are." With a quick jerk of his forearm he sent the shotgun barrel flying. "You could get hurt."

Before she could catch her balance, he swung her around and took her prisoner with an armlock. It wasn't the hold he would have preferred, given his lustful inclinations, but she was a squirrely little thing, and he wasn't playing any more games with her.

"Are you telling me I made love to a sixteen-year-old girl?" he asked, pulling her flush up against his body. He already knew the answer, but he wanted to hear it from her, straight out of her sweet, lying mouth.

Annie couldn't even breathe, much less answer him. Her heart was rushing wildly, and for some strange reason, her thighs were trembling as if they were going to give way. She knew he was trying to frighten her, but no matter what he threatened to do, she couldn't tell him the truth. He was already questioning the validity of the marriage, and she didn't want to feed his doubts. Consummating a marriage implied commitment and responsibility. It bonded the man and woman as life partners. If he thought they hadn't made love, it would give him all the more reason to discount everything about their unorthodox union—and to refuse her request for help.

"When did we do it, Annie?" he said, his voice rough and sensual. "How did we do it?" He clamped a hand around her middle, and let it slide up possessively, crowding her breasts. "Let's hear what happened between you and me, Red. Every hot, sexy little detail. I want to be sure I lived up to my husbandly duties."

"It wasn't like that," she said, trying to make him

understand. "You were sick, burning up with fever. I had to find a way to bring down your temperature. I sponged you and held you when you went into convulsions. There were strong feelings between us, yes. But it was more than physical. You talked about your dreams. You even told me about how you'd bought this cabin and were planning to settle here."

"A man says things when he's delirious," Chase muttered. But he was struck by the emotion breaking in her voice. She was passionate. And she seemed to be genuinely, poignantly angry with him for not believing her, or perhaps for not remembering. Whichever it was, she spoke with such depth of feeling, he found himself almost wanting to believe her . . . even to believe that he might have fallen in love with her back then, made love with her.

She tossed her head, and her soft red hair flew, cascading against his face, triggering another resurgence of memory, but only in indistinct images. He couldn't hear what she was saying as she writhed gently in his arms and murmured meltingly in his ear, but she was a beautiful, clinging presence, an angel gone wild. She made him ache in some deep, lonely part of his body, ache from wanting her. He could feel the need building up inside him even now.

The strange vision made him want to see Annie Wells.

He released her, turning her around, searching her face. "What happened between us?" he said, struck again by how vibrant she was when she was aroused. And by how tiny she was compared to him. The top of her head barely reached his jawline, and the hands she'd flattened against his chest looked doll-like and ineffectual.

Her breath caught in with a sharp, shaking sound. "You believe me?"

"Answer me, dammit."

"Everything," she said softly, as though trying to find the words. "Everything happened between us. Heaven and hell. We nearly died, both of us. We lived out a lifetime in a few sweet, terrible days."

"But you were only sixteen," he said. "I couldn't have—"

"No, I was never sixteen. When you're born an exile, as I was, you grow up quickly."

There was a hushed quality to her voice that intrigued him. It wasn't so much sensual as confessional, as though she was telling him all of it in strictest confidence, as though the words were for his ears only.

"It wasn't a child who saved your life," she said.

But Chase was only half listening by that time. Now her eyes were speaking to him, and they were even more eloquent than her words. They were made of some strange blue vapor, hc decided. They were misted with enchantment, and he could feel himself being drawn in again. His awareness narrowed, blocking out the world, taking in only the irresistible signals her body was giving off. There was an urgent flutter in her throat, and her breath was rushing soft and sweet against the dark hair that curled from the open collar of his shirt.

But it was the message in her dreamy, half-desperate gaze that burned through his hesitation. It obliterated all the other confusing signals. It promised him a tantalizing taste of ecstasy. She was willing to do anything, he realized, whatever he wanted, even make love to him right there where they stood, if that would convince him she was telling the truth.

The allure of the moment nearly overpowered Chase. It dragged at him like some intoxicating, mind-altering perfume. She *was* an angel gone wild, innocence set ablaze by her need and will.

"If it really happened," he said, fighting the pull, "if we really did make love, then tell me about it. Show me."

A glimpse of fear shadowed her expression. And then it was gone, as quickly as a summer cloud. Fear and desire, Chase thought, were a potent combination. He combed his hand into her hair, lifting it away from her face, aware of its weight and density despite the baby-fine texture. It felt like warm, heavy silk on his skin.

Chase hadn't intended to kiss her so quickly. It was even possible he hadn't intended to kiss her at all, but the slight quiver in her lower lip wrenched the decision away from him. The fluttering was barely discernible, but it was the damnedest, sexiest thing Chase had ever witnessed. There were some things a man just had to know, even when his common sense told him he'd be better off innocent. *What would all that trembling sweetness feel like under his mouth?* That was the question Chase had to have answered. Immediately.

She tilted up her chin as he bent to kiss her . . . but still it felt like an unbearably long, sweet time before their lips touched. Her mouth was even softer than he'd imagined, and a wild urge ran through him as he buried his hands deep in her hair and pulled her closer. God help him, he wanted to do what she swore he already had done. He wanted to get into those blue jeans of hers, badly.

She relaxed against him, murmuring something that might have been his name. Her breasts nestled his rib cage, and her hips came up against his, gently nudging. It was the softest kind of seduction, but it sent an impulse slamming through Chase that was as fierce and primitive as anything he'd ever felt in his life. The thunder of horses' hooves was pounding in his head and his chest, and he was getting hard. All he could think about was picking her up and settling her onto the rigid heat that sprang from his thighs, letting her ride him like a wild angel astride a renegade stallion.

"I want to make love to you, Annie," he said, his voice thick with desire. "I want to lift you up and take you in my arms. Right here, right now. What do you say to that?"

Desire flared in her eyes, and then they went smoky with fear. Her gaze said yes and no and maybe all at once. It said take her now, *quickly*, before she changed her mind and the fear won out.

The wrench of excitement deep in Chase's groin was almost painful. It told him he was running out of control. A distant voice was urging him to rein himself in while there was still time. And some part of him wanted to heed the warning. He actually wanted to stop, but he couldn't. He'd been taken captive by the telltale heartbeat in her lips. By the soft whimpers of pleasure in her throat.

"I must be dreaming," she said, her voice shaking oddly.

He broke away from her and dragged in a long, deep breath. She might be dreaming, but she was trembling, too, he realized. It had spread from the tantalizing quiver in her lower lip throughout her whole body, a near-violent tremor that he didn't know whether to attribute to fear or excitement. Her responses confused and excited him, the clinging lips, the sounds of pleasure. She was behaving like a woman who wanted to be bedded. And she was clutching at him almost possessively, the way a woman would cling to a man she hadn't seen in a long time.

As much as Chase wanted to shove aside all the conflicting signals and act on the urges that were making his body sing with need, something held him back. She was quaking like a willow branch caught in chinook winds, but that wasn't the only thing telling him to slow down. The static in his head was getting louder by the moment. The little voice had become a loud one, and it was telling him he was about to make one of the biggest, hairiest mistakes of his life.

Whether or not she was telling the truth was beside the point. As far as he could remember, he'd never set eyes on Annie Wells before. Worse, she was claiming to be his wife. Making love to her was bound to complicate things in that regard. At the very least she would see it as an admission on his part.

"Annie," he said, his voice tellingly hoarse as he freed his entangled hand from her hair. "Don't you think we might be rushing things a little?"

"Rushing things?" Even her chin was unsteady as she tried to smile at him and failed. She looked disappointed, a bit frightened, and very uncertain. "Do you think so? I guess we could slow things down, if that's what you want."

"If that's what *I* want?" Chase had to restrain himself from laughing out loud. "Just look at you, Red. You're shaking from head to toe."

She straightened her sweater, her fingers lingering at the neckline. "I'm probably only tired," she said, faintly apologetic. "I haven't slept in a while. Or eaten."

What's wrong with this picture? Chase wondered, staring at her hard. She was obviously frightened, exhausted, and probably starving. And yet she seemed more than willing to let him make love to her. She would undoubtedly go through with it right now if he pressed her. It didn't make sense. Unless she was hoping to accomplish something by offering him her body.

"Well, I'm not fine," he said, his suspicions deepening as he stepped back from her. He rubbed his forehead, aware of a lightheadedness that might have been pleasant if it weren't so distracting—and a warm, woozy feeling in the pit of his stomach. "If that rattler didn't get you, maybe it got me. I feel like I've been snakebit or something."

"Oh, I doubt that," she said, suddenly serious. "It's probably just that the blood has rushed from your head to that other part of your body—your male organ, I mean—and as soon as the blood begins to circulate again, your pressure will normalize and your brain will reoxygenate."

Chase managed a pained smile. "Excuse me?" That other part of his body she'd referred to was still as rigid as a crowbar. He could have opened a jammed door without using his hands, thanks in part to her. "How is it you know so much about the male . . . circulatory system?"

Annie smiled at his question. And at his long-suffering expression. He was breathtakingly sexy, even in his frustration. His face was as lean and hard as his body, and his glossy black hair had a dangerous way of spilling onto his forehead. Just to witness his reckless brand of sensuality could make a woman go weak, even at a distance.

"All good things come to those who wait," she thought, her smile deepening as she recalled one of the litany of proverbs she'd used to get herself through some very rough times in Costa Brava. How long had she waited to see him again like this?

"Do I get an answer?" Chase yanked his chambray shirt free of his jeans as he walked across the room to stand by a huge stone fireplace where the dog was snoozing.

"Oh, yes, it was my parents," she explained. "Remember I told you they were medical missionaries? Doctors? Well, they wanted me to be one too. They taught me themselves—the basics of medicine, of course, but everything else as well—math, English, American history."

She smiled suddenly, remembering. "The settling of the American West was the most exciting of all, don't you think? The Alamo, the Gold Rush in California, all of those cowboys and Indians. Did you know Wyoming is known as the Equal-Rights State? They had the first woman juror right here—"

She hesitated, blinking as Chase's features began to soften and fuzz around the edges. She backed up against the kitchen cabinet to steady herself, hoping it wasn't another dizzy spell. They'd been coming on for her with very little warning for the last couple of days. She knew it must be her blood sugar fluctuating wildly. She'd even fainted once or twice.

"You okay?" Chase asked.

"Yes," she said, bracing herself, determined to ward off the spell. In Costa Brava her world had been frighteningly unpredictable, and mastering her own physical weaknesses had given her at least a small measure of control.

"You were going to be a doctor?" Chase asked.

It took her a moment to make sense of his question, but when she did, her wan smile faded to sadness. "Yes, my parents were planning to send me to the United States to attend college when I came of age. It was their dream more than mine, but I understood why they wanted me to carry on the tradition. I would probably be in medical school right now if they hadn't been killed."

Chase inclined his head, nodding the way a man does when he hasn't got the right words. "That's tough," he said.

"It was . . . but it's been five years, and I've come to accept what can't be changed. My parents would have wanted that. They would have expected it."

A floorboard creaked under Chase's weight, and Annie automatically hushed her voice. It was a reflex she no longer seemed to have control over. "Is something wrong?" she asked, wondering why Chase was staring at her so oddly.

"Why do you do that?" he asked, studying her as he moved toward the table where he'd tossed his hat. "Talk in whispers?"

"Force of habit, I suppose. When you live in a convent, you learn to walk lightly and talk softly."

"A convent? In Costa Brava?"

She nodded. "That's where I've been these last five years." Except for the time I spent in prison, she thought.

"What kept you there? Your parents were gone. Why didn't you come to the United States?"

"There were many reasons." She considered telling him the whole painful story and decided it could wait. He'd had enough shocks in one day. "I wasn't there by choice at first, but then I came to see that I was needed," she said. "I taught Indian children to read and write. And in a war-ravaged country like Costa Brava, my medical skills were needed."

"A convent?" Chase asked, still intent. "At the tender age of sixteen? You were only a kid yourself." Curiosity stirred in his eyes. "What kind of things do they teach young girls in places like that?"

"Mostly survival, at first," Annie admitted. "Although Sister Maria Innocentia was also very big on the virtues of obedience, modesty, trust, and submission." She flushed slightly, realizing that might not be the wisest thing she could have revealed, especially since he was more than likely to mistake her meaning. "Of course, she also stressed prudent self-reliance."

Chase didn't respond other than to scoop his black Stetson off the table and slap it against his leg a couple of times, popping the dents out. But the faintest of smiles was prowling his normally taciturn features, and Annie knew he must be mulling over what she'd said.

"What do you do here?" she asked, hoping to head off any more questions about convent living. "In the way of work?"

Chase settled the Stetson on his head, letting it ride low in front so that the brim dipped even with his eyebrows. Equally dark hair swept over his ears and converged in a flurry of curls at the back of his neck. "I do some work for the Cattleman's Association," he said.

"You raise cattle?"

"No, nothing like that. I provide protection for the local ranchers." Chase couldn't see any reason not to tell her what he'd been doing since he settled in Wyoming. He was virtually certain by now that she wasn't a reporter, and if she was who she claimed to be, there was all the more reason to let her know how dirty and dangerous his work could be. No woman he'd ever known wanted her man tracking down cattle rustlers.

"I guess you could call me a range detective. When a ranch needs extra security, they hire me to patrol the area, or stake it out if necessary. But mostly I track down rustlers with prices on their heads. That's called bounty hunting."

She looked genuinely surprised. "They still have rustlers in Wyoming? Have you caught many?"

"A few," he said, glancing at the shotgun lying on the kitchen floor. He picked up the gun, emptied the shell from the chamber, and reinserted it in the magazine. "Got one today, but Bad Luck Jack doesn't count. He's meaner than a nest of rattlers, but he's also dumb, which makes him predictable. He spends more time in the slammer than out."

"Bad Luck Jack?" Annie said, laughing. "Doesn't sound like much of a challenge for a tough hombre like yourself."

"Hombre?" Chase winced. "What'd you do for entertainment in that convent? Watch B-westerns?"

"No, but I read a lot of western novels. My dad took a trunkload of them with him when he went to Costa Brava—and thank heaven he did. They were the only books we had other than his medical journals and my textbooks." She indicated Chase's hat and shot gun with a nod of her head. "Are you going somewhere?"

Chase shrugged. "I've been on a four-day stakeout, I'm fresh out of supplies, and you look like you could use some food. I was thinking about going into town to stock up, but I'll be damned if I can figure out what to do with you."

"Take me with you?"

She looked so hopeful, Chase almost wished he could. "Nope, that won't work." He'd purposely kept a low profile on his visits to town because he didn't want to give the locals reason to get curious about him. A female stranger riding shotgun in his Jeep was sure to draw attention.

"Why don't you get some rest," he suggested. "There's a shower if you want to take one."

"Oh, yes!" she said, an imploring quiver in her voice. "A shower? That would be heaven."

Chase had an involuntary flash of Annie Wells stripping and stepping into his makeshift shower. After their close encounter moments before, he knew better than to let his imagination take off in the direction of her shedding clothes. She was incredibly responsive, and he was no saint, especially where willing women were concerned. And yet, despite his concerted effort to banish it, the forbidden mental glimpse of her lithe, naked body created a hot spot in the pit of his stomach and raised goose bumps on his arms. It also gave him an idea.

"Take off your clothes, Annie."

"What?"

He tipped the shotgun barrel toward the ripped-out knee of her jeans. "Those dungarees, your sweater and shoes—take them off."

"Why?"

"You won't be needing them in the shower."

She brought a hand to her chest protectively. "Yes, I will," she insisted. "In the convent we always bathed in our clothing—at the very least, our shifts. Nudity wasn't considered proper."

Chase didn't know whether to chuckle or groan. She really was one for the record books. Not ten minutes ago she'd been ready to make babies with him. Now she wouldn't even take off her tennis shoes.

"Okay, then," he said, demonstrating what he thought was remarkable patience. "Take off everything but your shift, whatever that is."

"What are you going to do?" she demanded, backing away from him as though he were some kind of psycho or rapist.

"Nothing like what you're thinking," he assured her. "I only want to make sure you stick around until I get back."

"I won't go anywhere, I promise."

In Chase's line of work promises were about as useful as rats in a bunkhouse. And unlike Bad Luck Jack, Annie Wells had proved to be totally *un*predictable. No, until he'd had an opportunity to check out her story and find out exactly who she was, he didn't want her going anywhere or talking to anyone. He could just see the tabloid headlines if those sharks got hold of her. FORMER PENTAGON HERO STASHES AWAY CHILD BRIDE. Even the local papers would have a field day with that.

Back in their glory days, when Chase and his former partners were rescuing POWs and terrorists' hostages, they'd been made celebrities by the press. The media dubbed them "the Stealth Commandos" for their unorthodox methods of liberating American citizens, and the public's response promptly made heroes out of them.

Since the three men were single and eligible, the paparrazzi stalked them, hungry for news of their personal lives. Chase himself had been relatively free of the limelight since he'd retired to the wilds of Wyoming, but his former partners were still big news. Johnny Starhawk was a brilliant and controversial civil-rights lawyer, and Geoff Dias continued to run recovery missions.

No, Chase couldn't take the risk of letting Annie out of his sight until he knew what she was up to. He had the feeling she was an undetonated minefield, just waiting for someone to tread on her.

"Chase—" Her voice was hushed again, as though she'd been caught whispering during a church sermon. "I thought of something. What about the other two men, your partners? Why don't you contact them? They could tell you who I am."

His partners? She had to mean Johnny and Geoff. "How do you know them?" he asked.

Her blue eyes were sparkling with anticipation, as though she'd found the solution to all their problems. "We met with them on the way to the border, don't you remember? It was part of the plan, to discuss strategy. They'd found the scientists, and you'd found me. I even remember Johnny joking that you had the best deal."

Chase wondered why he hadn't thought of it. He didn't recall the meeting, but his partners had mentioned it briefly when they'd visited him in the hospital. They'd said very little about the girl, but Chase had assumed it was because of the tragic way she'd died. Later on, since no official agency had been able to find any record of her, the incident was pretty much swept under the rug.

The whole episode had left a bad taste in Chase's mouth. It had prompted his decision to retire, and then, in a dominolike reaction, that decision created a misunderstanding between him, Johnny, and Geoff. He hadn't seen either of his partners in over four years.

"I'm sure they'd remember me, if they saw me."

Annie's voice broke into his thoughts, soft and eager. "They had an Indian guide with them," she went on. "Only no one could understand him, so I interpreted. . . ."

Chase studied her as she recounted the story, searching her guileless features for any sign of deceit. The eagerness in her expression tugged at him, and he had to remind himself forcibly that the situation had been reversed only moments before. But she did have a way about her that made him want to abandon all his concerns, brave any danger, and gallop full tilt to her rescue. She *was* a land mine, he realized. And he was the idiot about to tread on her.

"At the very least they could verify who I am," she pressed. "Then would you believe me?"

"Maybe . . ." He drew up the barrel of the gun as he spoke, letting it point lazily in the vicinity of her thighs. A smile, faintly bemused, drifted over his face as he considered her flushed cheeks and the quick rise and fall of her breasts. She was an eyeful when she was excited. Obedience, modesty, trust, and submission, he thought, remembering the list of virtues she'd mentioned. He would soon know which, if any, Annie Wells had learned.

"But that isn't our immediate problem, is it?" he said, lowering his voice intentionally as he nodded toward her ragged sweater. "Come on now, Miss Annie. Don't make me have to do it for you. Take off those clothes."

Three

"Go ahead then," Annie said softly, dropping her clenched hand to her side. "Shoot me where I stand. Because I'm not going to undress at gunpoint. Not for you. Not for any man."

The words felt good as Annie said them, as sure and steady as she could ever have wanted them to be. But she'd barely had a chance to savor her potent declaration when she realized her misstep. She'd forgotten to take into account his reaction.

The look that crossed Chase's face at that moment would have given a corpse cause for concern. A corner of his mouth curled back in disbelief, and his black eyes narrowed to shimmering slits. *Anthracite,* she thought, aware that she'd finally come up with an apt description of his eyes. At the moment they looked hotter than the coals of hell.

"You've got it wrong, Red," he said. "I wasn't giving you a choice. Either you do the honors or I'll do them for you."

Annie's heart was beating hard enough to knock her to the floor, but she held his gaze without flinching. "Pull the trigger then," she said, raising her hands. "Shoot me and have it over with."

He shifted the gun, and Annie gasped. But instead of raising it to his shoulder, he dropped the weapon to his side, resting the butt end on the floor like a soldier on guard duty. "You're sure about that, Missy? You're willing to die?"

She gave him the nod every cowboy understands, just the slightest inclination of her head. She could tell by his expression that he'd cocked an eyebrow, although she couldn't actually see because everything above his hellfire eyes was covered by his low-riding Stetson.

"Would you like last rites?" His voice had gone dry as the dust coating his cowboy boots. "I'm not a priest, but I could hose you down or something."

Annie breathed a little easier at his sardonic tone. At least he hadn't put a bullet through her. Yet. "Last rites won't be necessary," she informed him quietly, lowering her hands. "I'm not actually Catholic. My parents were Episcopalians, I think. They never exactly declared themselves one way or the other, but they were quite progressive in their beliefs. My dad even brought in a local witch doctor as a consultant on occasion, to make our patients feel at home—"

"Annie!" He slammed the gun butt against the floor, and Annie started as though he'd shot the thing. All traces of amusement had vanished from his features. "Quit stalling and ditch those clothes, dammit."

Dizziness swamped her as she shook her head. "No! Not at gunpoint."

"Is this gun pointing at you, Missy?"

He did have her there, she realized. It was a technicality, but he had met her demand. He'd bent a little, and gut instinct told her that bending didn't come easily to Chase Beaudine. Still it galled her that he felt it necessary to take such extreme measures.

"Oh, all right," she said finally, impatience overriding her principles. "But this is so unnecessary. Where would I be going after traveling thousands of miles to find you?"

She yanked up her sweater and shift, and began to unsnap her jeans. "Go outside, will you?" she said, waving him toward the door. "Since you're leaving anyway I'll hand the clothes out when I'm done."

Chase caught himself about to turn toward the door and stopped short. *Damn, if she didn't have a bossy mouth on her.* Of all the virtues she'd been taught, apparently obedience hadn't had the slightest effect. "Watch the sass," he said, shooting her a black stare. "Or I'll have you peel down to the skin."

"I was planning to." Her eyes held a flash of defiance, but her voice revealed a soft, husky quaver he would have called seductive in another woman.

He watched in taut silence as she worked open the metal snap of her jeans and began to inch down the zipper, releasing the tiny teeth one notch at a time. She was either stalling again or deliberately taking her time to torture him. Whichever it was, she had a natural talent for annoying him.

"You want me to finish that for you," he warned, his hand tightening on the gun barrel, "just keep it up."

She drew the zipper down angrily, exposing a triangle of pink skin. As she dug her thumbs inside the waistband of her jeans and began to pull them down, Chase felt an odd clutch of sensation in his stomach. She wasn't wearing underwear! He was going to be seeing a lot more pink skin any minute now.

But instead of taking off the jeans, she left them hanging open, riding the rise of her slender hipbones, provocatively unzipped. And then, seemingly unmindful of Chase, she began to concentrate on unbuttoning her sweater.

Chase was anything but unmindful. It was one of the most riveting sights he'd ever been audience to. As her fingers worked open the tiny buttons, revealing creamy flesh and the promise of shivering female curves, he felt muscles deep inside him grab and yank tight, as if he'd been lassoed and jerked off his feet.

Sweet God in heaven. What was she doing? A

striptease? The woman was fresh out of a convent, by her own account. "Annie, what are you—"

"I'm almost done," she assured him, working diligently on the last of the buttons.

It looked as though she had on some kind of flimsy cotton camisole underneath the sweater, but that was it as far as Chase could see. Nothing else under there but the lush softness of a woman's body. Her full breasts were being crowded by her efforts to undress, and the result was an abundance of peek-aboo cleavage.

Chase winced at the explosive surge of energy in his groin. Did she have any idea what she was doing to him? In another damn minute he was going to have to excuse himself.

She looked up, her expression suffused with something that he might have called innocence if he hadn't been getting suspicious about her motives.

"Am I going fast enough for you?" she asked.

She was going just fast enough to make him wonder if a man had ever been put out of his misery because of unrequited lust. If you've got a problem now, cowboy, he thought sardonically, what are you going to do when she's naked? It was a moot question. He would never last that long.

Once she'd negotiated the last button and let her sweater fall open, she looked up at him. A radiant flush was creeping up her neck, and it was also wending downward, setting fire to her ample breasts. But it was the sparkle of apprehension in her eyes that caught hold of Chase's imagination and twisted it inside out.

With her burnished hair and blue eyes, she looked like an exotic moth who'd wandered into a spider's web and was trying to figure out what the big bad spider was going to do next. The whisper of alarm in her gaze, the excited quiver in her breathing, dealt a devastating blow to Chase's willpower. They aroused him even more than the lush innocence of her body. What was worse, she'd obviously aroused herself as well.

"I guess I'd better take off my jeans," she said, her voice catching slightly as she touched her fingers to her thigh. There was a hesitance in her manner that implied she was waiting for something. . . . His response? The shimmer of her breasts as she breathed, the question still trembling on her parted lips, all suggested that she would do whatever he told her to do, that she awaited his bidding.

Chase's mind shouted an answer. *Tell her to get her sweet butt out of those jeans and onto the cot behind her. Then give her exactly what her baby-blue eyes have been asking for. A joyride she will never forget.* The raunchy thought hit him with the sudden impact of a kidney punch.

"Was that a yes?" She began to tug down the jeans.

The moment of truth, Chase thought. If he let all hell break loose and acted on his impulses, he would undoubtedly feel a whole lot better afterward. And from the look of her, she would too. But would she let it go at that? Or would she see their lovemaking as some kind of commitment on his part? The very fact that he had to ask the question made it too big a risk. But then again, if he had to stand there and watch her drop her jeans without touching her, he was going to blow out like an overinflated tire.

"Hold it," he said, stopping her before the jeans could reach her hips. "I'm calling a time-out. In fact, I'm getting out of here while both of us are still vertical."

He wheeled and headed for the door. "I'll be on the front porch. You can hand your clothes out when you're done. And leave that shift thing on, for God's sake."

Annie watched, startled, as he slammed the door behind him. He'd certainly picked an odd time to make an exit. Her lack of experience in such matters left her a little bewildered, but she was burning up with curiosity. A faint smile blossomed as she stared at his escape route, the closed door. Had she actually run Chase Beaudine off? Was that possible? She hoped it was her fatal allure that had done it, rather than something else, such as the possibility that he didn't find her attractive, or Lord forbid, that he had some personal hang-up about sex.

Neither seemed likely since he'd wanted to make love to her earlier. But even then his behavior had been odd. He'd stopped in the middle of kissing her, insisting they were rushing things. She'd already sensed that he didn't have much use for women, especially a woman claiming to be his wife, but that alone couldn't account for his strange actions.

Annie's quandary increased as she glanced down. Half-dressed, she was startlingly sexy. What was the man's problem? Sex? Women? Annie Wells? Or all three?

Outside on the porch Chase waited impatiently for Annie to hand out the clothes. His only problem at that moment was putting some distance between himself and the frustrating female in his cabin. Maybe then he could get his blood pressure normalized and his brain "reoxygenated" before he became permanently addled. Given some thinking time, he told himself, a man could handle any woman, even one combat-trained in a convent.

"I'm still waiting for those clothes, Missy," he called, giving the door a kick.

"'All good things come to those who wait,'" she muttered a moment later as she handed out her jeans and sweater. "Happy?" she asked, plunking her tennis shoes on top of the pile and shutting the door with a sharp crack.

Happy? As he stared at the clothes, his mind scrolled image after lurid image of the woman who no longer wore them. No, happy wasn't the *H*-word that came to mind.

A flash of light bounced off Chase's side mirror, drawing his attention from the highway ahead. He slowed the Bronco, glanced over his shoulder, and glimpsed furtive movement out in the pasturelands.

He cranked the steering wheel hard and spun the Bronco into a 180-degree turn.

Gunning the four-wheel-drive vehicle, he drove it over the runoff ditch on the side of the road, then negotiated an obstacle course of underbrush and small trees as he sped toward the McAffrey ranch's lower pasture. Cattle thieves had been hitting the local ranches he provided security for, but these weren't penny-ante operators like Bad Luck Jack. This was a slick, big-time operation. Over the last few weeks they'd got away with several hundred head without leaving a trace.

Another flash of light caught Chase's eye as he spotted a lone figure some three hundred feet away, hunkered down next to a stretch of barbed-wire fence. Chase's savage desire to catch the bastards who'd been eluding him made him fearless—and reckless.

As the Bronco broke through the trees onto the open range, the man saw Chase and reared up. The rustler snarled an obscenity, then broke and ran. Chase hit the brakes and slammed out of the Bronco even before it had stopped moving. Bullwhip in hand, he sprinted in hot pursuit. By the time he'd gained enough ground to use the whip, his lungs were burning for air.

The man glanced over his shoulder as Chase closed in. With a roar of rage he heaved something sharp and metallic at Chase. Chase swerved as the glinting missile sliced open his shirtsleeve without tearing any flesh. A wire cutter, he realized, not a knife.

Chase shook out the fourteen-foot rawhide thong, bringing it up and back in one fluid, lethal arc of motion. He put the end of the whip exactly where he wanted it, around the slimy bastard's ankles. The man lurched forward, and Chase flipped the whip handle to his left hand. As he pulled the rawhide tight, he reached for the pump-action twelve-gauge he'd slung over his shoulder. He cocked the shotgun with one hand, a trick he'd learned in the military, and jammed the gun butt up against his shoulder as he approached the grounded man. "Who are you?" Chase demanded. "And what are you doing on McAffrey property?"

"I work here!" the man screamed, thrusting out an arm as though warding off demons. "I was riding fence, that's all."

Chase held him at bay, taking in the man's wiry, sweat-slicked features and wild-eyed fear. "Mending fences, my ass. Why the hell did you run?"

"Who wouldn't run with a maniac like you chasing him?" the man said, rubbing a grimy shirtsleeve over his dripping brow. "If you don't believe I work here, ask the foreman. He hired me yesterday."

Chase didn't like anything about the situation. He could smell a liar, and this bastard stank like hell on housecleaning day. He shook some slack into the whip and motioned the man to his feet. "Let's go have a talk with your foreman."

"Come here, Shadow," said Annie, trying to coax the Border collie away from his post by the cabin door, where he'd been waiting ever since his master left. The dog regarded her with wary disapproval, as though he were holding her responsible for his master's disappearance at the very least, and perhaps for any number of other things.

Glancing around the cabin, Annie shivered a little at its austerity. A large stone fireplace dominated the main room, and the few pieces of furniture Chase had were of sturdy white pine. Other than a couple of rifles hanging above the fireplace, there was nothing on the walls—no pictures, no curtains on the windows, no touches of color anywhere to alleviate the grayish expanse of unfinished wood. The place had all the severity of a monastery and none of the charm, she decided.

For some reason Shadow chose that moment to break his vigil. As Annie crossed the room to take a closer look at the kitchen area, the dog fell in behind her, sniffing at her legs and bare feet. Annie let him inspect her until he seemed satisfied, then reached down to stroke the silky black hair on his muzzle.

The cabin's kitchen was a little homier than the rest of the place, she noticed. A blue metal coffeepot with white speckles sat on a two-burner wood stove, and a red checkered oilcloth covered the small dinette table. The kerosene lanterns hanging from wall spikes made her think of scenes she'd read in her father's western novels, of winter storms when the snow heaped up to the eaves of a cabin's roof.

Shadow brushed her leg, seeking her attention, and his cool, wet nose startled a chuckle out of her. "Aren't you a friendly fella all of a sudden," she said, scratching the white patch on his head. The dog whimpered softly, and she crouched impulsively to give him a hug, surprised at the welling of emotion she felt. It was bittersweet and yet soft at the edges, an odd kind of yearning that seemed to concentrate in her arms, moving her to hug him tighter. She nuzzled into his ruff a moment and then released him, laughing as he began to lick her face. He was quivering with affection, and it was the first warmth Annie had experienced since she'd started her desperate journey. Lord, it felt good to have someone want her around. It felt almost like coming home. Or what she imagined that would be like. She'd never had anything resembling a normal home life.

Her eyes were misty as she sat on the floor next to the dog and surveyed the cabin again. If only the place weren't so cold and forbidding. It wasn't at all the house she'd been seeing in her mind all these years. She'd envisioned it as a picturesque log cabin with a tiny kitchen all fixed up with yellow curtains and ruffled seat cushions, a shaft of morning sunlight drifting through the window, warming a knotty-pine breakfast nook.

And of course she'd imagined herself in that kitchen, cooking up a mess of ham and eggs for breakfast. And the man of the house? Her cowboy lover? She closed her eyes, remembering the sweetest part of the dream for her. He would be out back splitting logs for firewood, probably shirtless and sweat-sheened, working up an appetite. After he'd washed up, he would want to steal a kiss, of course, and probably something more, but she would remind him that his sunny-side-up eggs were getting cold.

"I sure got it wrong, didn't I, Shadow?" She leaned into the dog's furry warmth for comfort as another lonely kind of aching flared up inside her. "This place isn't at all what I expected. And neither is he."

Shadow whimpered sympathetically and nuzzled her face.

"Thanks," she told the dog, smiling sadly as she accepted his condolences. "It's sweet of you to want to help, but the problem is bigger than both of us, I'm afraid. Your master doesn't seem to remember me. Or maybe he doesn't want to."

She drew the dog close again, warding off the panic that was stirring inside her. What would she do if Chase refused to help her? She couldn't throw herself on the mercy of the Immigration and Naturalization Service. She'd heard all the horror stories about illegal aliens being held in compounds for months, then shipped like cattle back to wherever they'd come from. And even if the stories weren't true, she almost certainly wouldn't be allowed to stay in the country if she couldn't prove her citizenship.

A chill washed over her like an icy bath of water. Sent back to Costa Brava? After the nightmares of the last five years? She released the dog and pushed to her feet, fighting a wave of dizziness that crested so suddenly it threatened to drag her under. "I can't let that happen, Shadow. No one's going to send me back there."

Chilled through to the marrow, she made it over to the cot and pulled the quilt coverlet around her. How long had it been since she'd eaten? Hours? Days, maybe? She was losing track of time again. Everything was blurring together. A seductive kind of lethargy was seeping through her muscles and bones, dragging her down into the sweet oblivion of sleep. The sheer weight of it had overwhelmed her before. She'd slept in parks and bus terminals, drugged by exhaustion. She supposed it was a variation on the fainting spells, but she couldn't let herself give in to the heaviness now. She had to stay awake, stay focused. She had to find a solution to her problem.

"What am I going to do?" she said, as the dog came over to sit before her. He looked up at her eagerly, but his huge brown eyes were so sad and sympathetic, they filled her with despair. Finally he rested his muzzle in her lap, and it seemed as if the two of them sat that way for a long time.

Consummation? The word came to her in a burst as she huddled in the threadbare quilt material. It created such a shimmering explosion of awareness inside her that she felt as if the reference must have been sent to her through some kind of divine intervention.

"Consummation," she murmured aloud, testing the word's susurration on her tongue, and getting a sense of its deeper significance as she let the awareness take on meaning and shape. Suddenly she knew what had to be done. She knew!

With a quick smile she glanced up. "Thank you."

Shadow's tail was wagging so hard by that time, it shook his whole body. Annie scratched his ruff, excitement growing inside her, reviving her. "You know it, too, don't you, Shadow? You understand that I'm going to have to seduce your master. There's no other way."

Her heart began to pound recklessly as she considered the possibilities. Seduce Chase Beaudine? Could it be done? Was there a woman alive who could bend that iron man's will and make him want her enough to succumb? Perhaps it was wishful thinking, but something inside her needed to believe that making love would help Chase to remember their bond. He couldn't pretend she meant nothing to him once he'd made love to her, could he? He couldn't pretend she didn't exist.

Shadow began to whimper eagerly, and Annie realized she'd stopped stroking him in her preoccupation. "This isn't going to be easy," she said. "How do you seduce a man who refuses to be in the same room with you?"

Beyond Chase's obvious reluctance, she herself had a major handicap when it came to undertakings like seduction and consummation. She had no experience with men. None! At a time when most girls were learning to flirt, she had been teaching Indian children to read and write Spanish in a convent school. If she'd aroused Chase while undressing, that was a lucky accident. She wouldn't know how to seduce a man if he gave her step-by-step instructions, and Chase Beaudine didn't seem likely to do that.

"'Where there's a will,'" she said, abbreviating another of the proverbs she'd picked up from the sisters. Actually, Sister Maria Innocentia's advice had usually been a bit wordier. "Action must necessarily follow resolution if goals are to be achieved," the venerable mother superior was fond of saying.

Annie glanced up suddenly, searching the cabin with her gaze. Chase had mentioned a shower, hadn't he? She'd always done her best thinking in the convent's makeshift shower, and she badly wanted to get reacquainted with some warm water and a bar of soap. It had been so long.

Rising stiffly to her feet, she tugged at the short cotton shift that had once come down to her calves and was the regulation undergarment in the convent. After years of trying to tuck the voluminous thing into her jeans, she'd simply whacked most of the bottom off one day, much to the sisters' dismay. So as not to further offend their sensibilities, she'd left intact the words embroidered in pink thread across the bodice: VIRTUE IS ITS OWN REWARD.

She found the shower in a closet-sized bathroom off the hallway. The floor was wooden slats spaced wide for drainage, and the rusty shower head looked as if Chase had stolen it off the nozzle end of a hose. Not what she'd hoped for, but nothing could have dissuaded her from the prospect of cleaning up.

She turned on the tap and then jumped back with a startled cry as an icy jet of water hit her. It took several minutes for it to warm up, but when it did, she stepped into the stinging spray with great relief, shift and all.

It was heaven, pure bliss, she decided, scrubbing herself with a bar of gritty soap that smelled so strongly of lye it stung her nostrils. "Cleanliness and godliness," she murmured. "However that one goes."

Turning in the shower spray, luxuriating in its pounding heat, she could have stood forever in the soapy, steaming cocoon. But all the years of convent living and the impoverishment of her circumstances made her feel a little guilty about indulging herself now. She glanced down at her water-soaked shift and felt a pang of despair as she ducked her head under the spray. Was virtue really its own reward? she wondered, soaping her hair. And what chance did a woman with a platitude embroidered on her underwear have of seducing an unwilling man?

The black Ford Bronco's chassis bounced against taut springs, its engine snarling as Chase geared down and swerved to avoid a darting ground squirrel. The gravel access road that led to his cabin had ruts the size of small open graves and a pitch too steep for anything but a rugged four-wheel-drive vehicle.

Grocery bags Chase had forgotten to secure toppled over in the backseat as the Jeep jolted up the hill. There went the eggs, he thought, glancing in his rearview mirror. They'd be scrambled before he got back to his place. But he didn't bother to slow down. A blazing sunset had drenched the craggy mountain peaks ahead of him in coppery oranges and reds, which meant he had less than a half hour to get home before dark.

The slimy character Chase had apprehended on the McAffrey spread had turned out to be telling the truth. He was a newly hired hand, according to the foreman, who assured Chase the man had been sent out to mend fences.

Something about the situation still stank as far as Chase was concerned, but he'd let it go, apologized to the man for roughing him up, and headed into Painted Pony to pick up supplies. Then, before he'd left town, he'd tried to contact his former partners by telephone and hadn't been able to reach either of them. Johnny Starhawk was arguing an important case before the Federal District Appeals Court, and Geoff Dias was on a top-secret mission somewhere in the Middle East.

Chase had left urgent messages for both of them. He'd even used an old code word to alert them that his life depended on their quick response. They might not appreciate his tactics when they found out what was actually going on. But hell, it *was* his life at stake. He had a woman claiming legal rights to his bed and board, to his personhood!

He didn't like anything about the predicament with Annie Wells. And he especially didn't like the fact that he was in such a hurry to get back to her. Actually it wasn't Annie he was in a hurry over, he told himself. It wasn't the woman herself who had him worked up. It was all the emotional baggage she brought with her. She was a threat to his way of life, to his very peace of mind. He had to get things under control.

Not a second later, he had a graphic mental flash of the striptease she'd done in his living room, and he nearly veered off the road. He hit the brakes and brought the Jeep to a stop that sent gravel flying like shrapnel. A vein throbbed in his forehead as his own black eyes flashed hotly from the rearview mirror. Who are you kidding, you dumb ass? It's not the predicament you're hurrying back to. It's *her*.

• • •

The crimson sky was swathed in deep purple velvet by the time Chase pulled up to his cabin. Like a plush theater curtain dropping, it blotted out the footlights of the fallen sun. Unaware of the spectacular beauty around him, uncaring, Chase reached over the backseat and scooped up the grocery bags.

He thought he'd prepared himself for any eventuality when he nudged open the cabin door with his foot. He'd imagined her sound asleep on the cot, curled up like a kitten. Or long gone with all his possessions. He'd even imagined her staring down the barrel of a gun at him. But it had never occurred to him that she might be standing in the bathroom doorway naked and dripping wet.

"What the hell?" It was a moment before he realized she wasn't totally naked. She had on that flimsy, sliplike thing, but sopping wet, the material might as well have been invisible. Patches of it clung to her breasts and hugged the slender lines of her body in ways that were indescribably sweet, and unspeakably lewd.

Chase felt as though he'd been hit by a truck in high gear. She aroused feelings in him that were both carnal and impossibly innocent. She took him back to his teenage years. She made him yearn for young love. She made him remember the wet dreams and every dirty movie he'd ever seen—or wanted to see.

Set the groceries down, cowboy. Before you drop them.

He deposited the bags on the table by the cot, but nothing had changed when he turned back to her. She was still standing there, dripping all over his hardwood floor and staring at him like a wood nymph caught emerging from some magic pool. "Annie, what the hell—"

"I took a shower," she said, stating the obvious. She shifted her weight, a barely discernible movement that hung the diaphanous material over her thighs and hipbones like cellophane wrap, revealing a reddish delta of hair. Strawberries and cream, Chase thought, struck by the contrast of her ginger hair and her porcelain skin tones.

He could feel his breathing quicken as he stared at her. He could feel muscles responding and heat gathering. Luckily there was something stopping him from making wild love to her right there on the floor in a pool of water. It was the total incongruity of the situation.

The woman standing across the room from him didn't seen unduly embarrassed by having been caught naked, and yet she couldn't have had much experience with men if what she'd told him about the convent was true. She hadn't even been allowed to shower in the nude.

Sweet God, he thought. Could he actually have made love to her on that mission? If he'd been delirious, he wouldn't have known what he was doing, but still, she hadn't been much more than a child. She looked like a child even now with her damp copper-colored ringlets, cameo complexion, and grave, trusting expression.

"Get yourself dry, Annie," he said abruptly. "And get some clothes on."

"I don't have any clothes," she said. "You took them."

So he had. Chase glanced at his blue chambray shirt. A moment later he'd pulled off the shirt and was tossing it to her. "You can wear this," he said. "I'm going to put the groceries away."

The shirt dropped at her feet, and she stared down at it for a long time, but she made no attempt to pick it up. "I have a better idea," she said at last, her voice soft and trembling. "You could make love to me."

Four

Chase froze where he stood. He knew what he'd heard, but he didn't want to believe it. And yet the sparkle of fear in her eyes could as easily have been excitement. If he'd had a choice, he would have called a halt to the proceedings right there. But it was already too late for that. His blood pressure was on the rise. His stomach muscles grabbed, and an odd thrill sank deep into the muscles of his legs as he stared at her.

"Put on the shirt, Missy," he said, furious with her. And with himself.

She shook her head, looking more like a frightened, defiant child than a woman who wanted to make love. Chase grabbed the quilt off the cot, strode over to her, and draped it around her shoulders.

"Is there something wrong with me?" she asked, her voice strangely faint, her eyes sparkling with tears. "Am I too ugly? Too skinny?"

Chase told himself to let go of the blanket, to release her at once. Instead, his hands curled into fists, and the material tautened in his grip. "No, you're not ugly, Annie. A little skinny maybe, but that's not the problem."

He caught the clean, damp scent of her hair as she swayed toward him, the freshness of her skin. Her breasts bounced and strained against the wet fabric, her nipples hardening. And even as Chase ordered himself to let go of her, to back off, he knew it was too late to stop.

"You really want me to make love to you, Annie Wells?" he said, his voice going dry with desire. "You're bound and determined that's what you want?"

"Yes. That's what I want. . . ."

Annie left the last word whispered and dangling. She caught hold of his arms and tilted her head up, as though waiting to be kissed. Chase was aware of something slightly off-kilter in the focus of her eyes, and her smile was charmingly askew, but to a man with his overheated sensibilities, those signals registered as one thing only—dazed passion.

She obviously wanted to be kissed, but with the quilt tangled up in his grip and her clinging to him so urgently, it took some negotiating. She murmured unintelligibly as their bodies touched. Their lips brushed tentatively at first, and then, as the kiss deepened to something wild and breathless, she let out a soft, shocked moan, her eyes fluttered closed, and her body went suddenly, meltingly limp.

"Annie?" Chase caught her by the arms as she sank toward the floor.

"Oops," she murmured. "Sorry . . ."

Chase braced her on her feet and held her at arm's length, studying her pale features and drooping eyelids. He'd had some interesting responses to his advances over the years. He'd been slapped a few times, even kneed once, but nobody had fainted on him. What was it with this woman? He had half a mind to release her and let her fold up like an accordion. He might have done it, too, if she hadn't looked so deathly pale.

"Annie," he said, his voice harsh. "What seems to be the problem here?"

"No problem," she said, swaying in his hold. "Blood chemistry, I think—drop in glucose . . . haven't eaten."

He didn't doubt her last statement, but he still

wasn't convinced about the fainting-spell business. There was one way to find out, of course. "Can you stand up?"

She opened her dreamy blue eyes and nodded slowly.

"You mean it? Because once I let go, you're on your own."

Her response was another slow-motion nod, which Chase decided to take as a yes. He released her, unprepared as she actually sagged to the floor in a graceful heap.

Well, she wasn't faking it. With a taut sigh and a slow head shake, Chase stared down at her soft, crumpled form, wondering what he was going to do with her. With her arm flung out to her side, she looked fragile and very much abandoned, like an old-fashioned doll that some careless youngster had grown tired of and tossed away.

There was something about the woman lying at his feet, Chase realized, that caused bittersweet feelings to grow in him. Something almost heartbreaking written in her odd, delicate features, perhaps even in her nature. "Oh, Miss Annie," he said, his voice suddenly low and grating, "why do I have the feeling you're going to be the undoing of us both?"

She stirred as he knelt to pick her up. "Chase?" she said, rousing in his arms as he carried her to the cot.

"Easy does it." He settled her on the small bed and pulled the quilt snugly around her, hushing her as she tried to convince him that she was fine. "What you need is some food, Missy. How long since you've had a decent meal?"

Annie didn't have the energy to answer him, or to argue with him, for that matter. She could hardly keep her eyes open, much less try to persuade him that she really did want to make love with him, however unlikely that might appear. She'd known this day of reckoning was coming. A body could only endure so much punishment, and she'd pushed hers unmercifully.

She was pleasantly aware of Chase's touch as he patted her legs dry with the quilt material. He had a surprisingly gentle way for a hardened bounty hunter, and she was beginning to wish he would never stop tending to her needs when the cot creaked mournfully and he rose, leaving her.

"Here's a clean shirt," he said, returning a moment later. "You can put it on when you're feeling a little stronger."

She opened her eyes, managing a nod as he laid a faded chambray shirt next to her. The wariness in his expression had been replaced by something friendlier, something that could almost have been mistaken for tenderness as he looked down at her.

Annie felt a welling of emotion that expanded oddly in her throat. "Chase, I'm sorry. I thought . . . I didn't know I'd be causing all this trouble."

"No trouble," he said. "I think I can feed you without putting myself out too much."

He touched a forefinger to her face, just a fleeting stroke of kindness, but the gesture sent a rush of longing through Annie that was sharp and poignant. Some tiny blaze that had been kindling in her breast all those years flared higher, reaching out for his life-giving tenderness as though it were oxygen. Tears stung at her eyelids as she quickly squeezed them shut, uttering the only words she could manage: "Thank you."

Some time later, she wasn't sure how long, the delicious smells of frying meat, onions, and potatoes stole into her consciousness, awakening her. Chase stood at the two-burner stove, his back to her as she opened her eyes. He had a couple of cast-iron skillets going, and they were both sizzling and sending up clouds of steam.

Her mouth began to water, and her stomach seized up painfully, closing on its own emptiness. Fighting off dizziness, she pushed herself to a sitting position and stayed there a moment until she felt steady enough to try to change into the shirt he'd left her.

It took considerable effort to peel off the damp shift

and fumble her way into the shirt, particularly since she was determined to do it within the tentlike confines of the quilt. She had no desire to distract Chase. Now that she'd had a whiff of real food, the only sort of consummation she was interested in was at the dining table.

First things first, she told herself, redoubling her efforts to do up the shirt's buttons. Clearly it took considerable stamina to seduce an unwilling man, and she would have to get her strength up for the task. She certainly didn't want to keep fainting every time he got near her. They wouldn't get anything accomplished that way.

Moments later Chase set two bowls of steaming food and a loaf of warm sourdough bread down on the red checkered oilcloth. When he saw she was awake, he said, "Come and get it," pulled back a chair, and beckoned her.

He'd put his own shirt back on, but he hadn't bothered to button it up. The jeans riding low on his hips and dark hair curling down the nape of his neck made him look nonchalant and recklessly sexy. More like a gunslinger taking a break from the action than a mountain man who'd just cooked her dinner.

She rose to her feet unsteadily and noted with some relief that the shirt she wore was long enough to be a short dress. The tails fell practically to her knees.

"What's this?" she said as she sat down across from him.

"If you mean the food, it's corned-beef hash. Sorry, I don't do fancy."

"Looks like a feast to me," Annie said.

Those were her last words for some time. She ate voraciously, delaying each heaping spoonful only as long as it took to chew and swallow. When she was done, she glanced up, spoon still clenched firmly in hand, and saw that Chase hadn't eaten a bite. He'd been watching her with rapt disbelief, apparently the entire time.

She tipped her spoon toward his bowl. "Are you

going to finish that?" It seemed a sin to waste good food, especially since the mound of steaming ambrosia in his bowl was sending up an irresistible aroma.

He pushed the bowl over to her side of the table without a word. Annie could feel his eyes on her as she started in on his portion, and it occurred to her that the nuns would not have been pleased with her manners. At the very least she ought to have complimented Chase on his cooking skills or inquired on his lack of appetite. But she couldn't spare the time from her food. It seemed as if some ravenous, foraging animal had taken over her will. She was absolutely drunk on the mouthwatering smells and tastes. Consummation was a wonderful thing, she thought, smiling at the awareness. She felt as if she could consume Chase's corned-beef hash forever and never be full, never get enough to satisfy her hunger.

"*Exquisito*," she said, some moments later after she'd finished every morsel of the food and was polishing the inside of the bowl with a chunk of bread. "Really, it was exquisite. I've never had hash before. Is it a local delicacy?"

Chase nodded, a wry smile surfacing. "Ranks right up there with prairie chips and Rocky Mountain oysters. Remind me to whip you up a batch of those sometime."

"Oysters? Here in the mountains?" Annie couldn't restrain a skeptical headshake as she finished the last of the bread. "Wonders never cease," she murmured.

"No . . . they never do."

Something in his voice made her glance up, and as she did, she caught the fleeting appreciation that moved through his expression. A lightness buoyed her heart as she registered his recent kindnesses—and wondered what they meant. It seemed too good to be true that he might have changed his mind and decided to help her prove her citizenship. She'd lived so many years in a country ripped apart by insurrection that deprivation and fear had become a way of life. She'd thought of herself as inured to the pain. And yet now, even anticipating that the nightmare might be over brought her a sense of relief so powerful, it felt almost joyous.

"You get enough?" Chase asked, glancing at the empty bowls and bread crumbs, the only evidence that there'd been food on the table. "Looks like I should have thrown a side of beef on the stove."

"Oh, no." Annie settled back in the chair and allowed herself a deeply contented sigh. "Don't bother, really. I don't think I could eat another bite. What about you?"

He grinned ruefully at the empty bowls and tilted back in his chair, his unbuttoned shirt falling open. "I'm watching my figure," he said, cocking his head in a way that made his powerful neck muscles stand out.

Annie was riveted by his tone of voice. She didn't know how to describe it except that there was an undercurrent of sensuality in his cowboy drawl that had her feeling faint all over again. She knew without doubt that if he ever spoke words of love to her in that slow, rusty voice, even if all he said was "Come here, Annie," she would have no choice but to go. He would own her, body and soul.

"Your figure looks fine to me," she said, drawing in a breath as she surveyed the muscular landscape that his open shirt revealed. She supposed she ought to be blushing and fanning herself at the sight of so much naked masculinity. It seemed like a natural enough inclination, and probably what a woman intent upon seduction would do. But now that she'd noticed his body, she simply couldn't take her eyes off it.

His upper torso looked as hard and unforgiving as the badlands she'd just crossed. His skin glowed with burnished gold tones that made her think he must have spent some time working without his shirt on. And the lean, aggressive flare of his stomach muscles were something to behold. A swath of chest hair dusted his pectorals and cut a narrow path toward his jeans, streaking like a dark river over sinewy ridges and planes.

The quickening beat of Annie's heart confused her. Raised as she had been among the Indians, she'd seen plenty of half-naked male bodies, some of them extremely well developed. And Chase Beaudine, magnificent as he might look at the moment, had basically the same equipment. Pectorals were pectorals, weren't they? The collarbone was still connected to the shoulder bone, no matter what the body looked like. And yet try as she would to analyze the situation dispassionately, nothing in her parents' anatomy and physiology texts had prepared her for the collarbones of the man sitting across from her.

"You sure you got enough to eat?" Chase interrupted her survey with an inquisitive smile. "If I hadn't seen you finish off two bowls of hash and a loaf of bread, I might think you wanted to start in on me."

Annie blinked with surprise, and the blush she hadn't been able to summon earlier swept her face and throat full force. "Chase Beaudine," she said softly, "what are you doing? Flirting with me?"

She did have an interesting way of putting things. Chase pushed back from the table, chair and all. The movement was as slow and deliberate as his feelings were hot and impulsive. There'd been enough "flirting" going on since he met her to make up for the last five years of his life. But he wasn't lighting the brushfires and sending up the smoke signals. She was. If ever a woman wanted to be taken advantage of, this one did.

"I think we're past the flirting stage," he said, his voice tellingly husky. It was plain where the conversation was headed, and common sense alone told him not to pursue it, but he couldn't resist. What red-blooded man could resist when the woman sitting across the table from him was wearing his work shirt and nothing else? Besides, he was almost beginning to like the challenge of seeing how far he could go with her and still pull back. There was something irresistibly seductive about walking that close to the edge. Maybe it was a sad comment on his life these days, but very little else made him feel so alive, except possibly staring death in the eyes.

"Past flirting?" She shifted nervously and tried with no success to smooth back her hair. "What stage are we in then?"

"I don't know. The getting-down-to-it stage, maybe?"

"Getting down to it?" She stared into his eyes for several seconds, and then her shoulders rose as she took a deep breath. "What does that mean exactly?"

"You want the truth?"

After a moment of hesitation, she nodded.

"It means that ever since you sat down, I've been thinking about lifting those shirttails of yours and using this table for a bed." He watched her breathing quicken and her color go from deep pink to scarlet. Without any effort at all Chase could imagine sweeping all the dishes aside, picking her up, and laying her down on the cool, slick oilcloth.

He tipped back, his creaky wooden chair precariously balanced on its back legs. The scene flashed through his mind . . . her hair in wild disarray as she opened her arms to receive him, her fingers tangling urgently in his hair . . . her thighs soft and opened, inciting passion, and both of them too crazy with desire to bother with preliminaries.

A sheen of sweat broke out on his brow at the imagined pleasure. Things were getting crazy again, he told himself. He was getting crazy. But what amazed him most about his reaction to her was the defection of his legendary willpower. He'd never had a problem controlling himself with women. He'd gone without sex for months at a time on a mission, just because it seemed like more trouble than it was worth. But with her he was like a stallion waiting to be led to stud.

"Right here?" she said softly. "On the table?"

"I'm thinking about doing things that'll make your

toes curl, Annie. Pleasures so sweet, they'll make you want to die just a little."

"Die? On the table?" She raised a hand to her forehead as though she were trying to visualize such a thing. "Oh, my word," she said, her voice thready and light. "Couldn't we just—"

Chase's eyes swept over what he could see of her body, searching out the gentle swing of her breasts beneath the loose shirt. It was time to pull back from the edge, he told himself. His nerve endings were flashing messages, thickening his muscles and teasing his senses with signals. His vision sharpened until he thought he could see her nipples hardening against the cotton material. His hearing was honed for the sexy rasp of her breathing. *It's time, cowboy. Head off the thundering herd before it goes over the cliff.*

But his heart was pounding like a jackhammer, and the darkening pull of her eyes was irresistible. He let the chair legs drop to the floor as he stood up. "Couldn't we just do *what,* Annie? You got a problem with doing it on the table?" he asked softly. "You're not sure you want it that rough-and-ready?"

Her fingers whitened against the edge of the table as she looked up at him. She could hardly get the words out. "I am sure, yes . . . I—I do want that. If you do."

Her vulnerability enflamed his desire. She was so nakedly willing to do whatever he asked of her that Chase felt a gut-punch of animal passion. Wonder and anger and violent need all raged inside him. God, he wanted her. He was *crazy,* wanting her.

He hit the chair with his leg, accidentally knocking it over. The clattering noise gave him the briefest jolt of satisfaction, and then he met her gaze. Her blue eyes were wide with alarm. She was obviously shocked by his suggestion, maybe even a little frightened, but still she was willing to go along with it. Why? What kind of cosmic joke was this? Who in the hell had sent Annie Wells to torment him?

He yanked the chair upright and slammed it to the

floor, consumed by a wave of self-disgust. He was furious at himself for what he'd done. And furious with her for what she was apparently willing to do. Good Lord, was she ready to sacrifice anything? Was her birthright, as she called it, worth that?

"What the hell are you doing, woman?" he asked softly. "Don't you know better than to bargain with bastards?"

He strode to the door and threw it open, needing the fresh, cool air. Heat was steaming through his veins and rising off the back of his neck as he stood on the threshold. Right. You tell her about bastards, cowboy, he thought acidly. You just do that little thing. Stink up the room with your nobility.

There was no equal distribution of blame in this situation. He was clearly the only bastard in sight. It was his fault, all of it, but knowing that didn't make him any less angry. And it didn't stop him from wanting to rail at the whole damn world. What kind of system was it where people like his parents had nothing better to do than abuse alcohol to the point of nearly killing each other? And what kind of madmen butchered a young girl's parents and forced her into hiding?

What kind of woman traded her body for her birthright?

He turned back to her, ready to lash out, but he was struck silent by the bewilderment in her expression, by the glimmer of raw pain in her eyes. The truth hit him as he stared at her. She was a woman who'd had to survive, he realized, under the most brutal of circumstances. She'd done it by sheer endurance, and by a kind of surrender that he would never understand. She was the willow tree he'd once compared her to, fragile but enduring, with a root structure that would allow her to bend but never to break. Her spirit had been tested. And she was strong, stronger than he would ever be.

But why was she looking at him that way? As though he'd just flung her dreams back in her face. He studied her features, drawn by the mix of anguish and urgency. There was something in her expression that wrenched him, a tiny sparkle of light that held him prisoner. Even the dull sheen of pain couldn't hide its stubborn glimmer. Hope, he realized. For God's sake! Despite everything, she was still holding out hope where he was concerned. Suddenly he understood what he had to do, and it was unbelievably cruel. He had to blunt that emotion in her eyes, or he would never be free of her hold.

"I've only got one thing to say to you, Annie—" His voice broke roughly, then hardened. "I'm not the white knight you've been dreaming about with those sky-blue eyes of yours. A man would have to be blind not to see all the wanting in you, all the yearning, but I'm not the one to satisfy it."

Dull red stained her cheeks, and Chase knew he had found the wellspring of her hope, and her pain. He turned back to the icy night sky, gripping the doorframe above him with one hand. "I'm not the hero you've been remembering, so get that straight. I'm not polite, and I don't ask nice. Especially when it comes to women. I see something I want, I help myself."

With a hard crack of his palm against the wood, he emphasized his words, then strode out to the porch and stood at the railing, his back to her. "So be warned, Annie Wells," he said, his harshness shattering the serenity of the mountain night. "Don't make me want you too much. You might not like what you get."

Annie's mouth filled with a bitter taste as she stared at his back. She felt betrayed, violated. How did he know she'd thought of him as the white knight, the rescuing hero? And why did he want so badly to hurt her? It made her feel foolish and debased to think she had imagined his strength, his gentleness. She'd convinced herself that she would treasure both qualities when she and Chase were finally reunited. But it would never be like that with Chase Beaudine, she realized. His soul *was* as dark as his eyes.

A chill gust of night air swept her bare legs as she forced herself to rise from the chair and walk out to the porch where he stood. His back was to her, and the physical power implicit in his neck and shoulders was enough to ward off any but the foolhardy. But Annie couldn't be warded off. She had nothing left to lose. "I'll leave then," she said. "That's what you want."

"No, Annie, that's not what I want."

His husky answer sparked a dying ember of hope, but she couldn't let herself respond to it. He would only take it away. He knew how to hurt her now.

"I want this matter of your identity cleared up," he said. "And until it is, I want you to do exactly as I say."

"What does that mean?" She waited, thinking he was going to turn around. He didn't.

"You and I aren't getting together, Annie—in any way. You can stay on here until Johnny or Geoff shows up, but that's as far as it goes."

"Johnny or Geoff? Your partners?" Annie reached out in surprise, then checked herself before touching his shirtsleeve. "Did you talk to them?"

"I couldn't reach them, but I left messages. They'll come."

"And if they verify my story?"

"I'll worry about that if it happens. In the meantime you just sit tight in this cabin, mind your own business, and don't speak to anyone. I'm a private man. If people knew I had a woman up here, they'd start talking, snooping in my personal life."

Annie thought it unlikely she would run into anyone to talk with, isolated as they were, but she was curious as to why he was so protective of his privacy. "Why would anyone care so much about your personal life?"

He whipped around and caught hold of her by the arm, yanking her close. "You got a problem with your hearing, woman? I said mind your own business."

His eyes were so ungodly black that Annie felt a moment of true terror. She'd seen him in action in

Costa Brava. He'd killed a man without flinching. Now he seemed more than capable, and perfectly willing, to use force to persuade her if necessary. "All right," she said. "Whatever you say."

Chase Beaudine was as good as his word in the days that followed. He *was* a bastard. Annie decided that if awards were given for making animal noises, he would win by a landslide. He grunted, growled, and snarled under his breath, letting his clothes lie wherever they dropped and slamming noisily around the cabin. If she made any mention of his surliness, he glared at her and told her to stop running her mouth.

His outrageous behavior infuriated her at times, but it also helped her put things in perspective. It reminded her that she'd faced far worse in Costa Brava. Grim despair and death were daily occurrences there. Everyone in the convent had been tested beyond the limits of most human endurance, and in comparison, Chase Beaudine's bad manners seemed about as painful as sitting on a hard pew in church.

Her promise to follow his rules was a different matter, however. It wasn't that he made impossible demands on her, it was more what he forbade her to do that chafed. Minding her own business, as he'd so succinctly put it, covered a lot of territory. She was eager to clean up the cabin, but he didn't even want her to dust. He was obsessive about her not "messing with his things." And when she offered to cook, he grudgingly gave his permission, so long as it was "meat and potatoes." He wasn't even willing to discuss getting special ingredients so she could try to adapt recipes for exotic Indian dishes she'd learned to make in the jungle.

Luckily he didn't seem to mind her whiling away the hours with Shadow, and occasionally he left the collie to keep her company while he investigated a cattle theft or rode fence on one of the ranches he provided security for.

So Annie entertained herself with throwing sticks for Shadow, and with taking long walks to pick wildflowers in the verdant meadows that bordered Chase's property. She also spent considerable time fantasizing about the Chase Beaudine she remembered, and how she would have turned his cabin into a cozy home—complete with flowers and sunny yellow curtains—if he'd given her the chance.

On one of her many sojourns to the meadows, she came across some trees bearing apples that looked similar to a variety they'd made wine from at the convent. Excited, she picked as much of the ripe fruit as she could carry, and immediately set to work on a wine-making project. Hoping Chase wouldn't notice it, she kept the glass jugs and siphon hose behind the toolshed.

She also added liberal amounts of Chase's whiskey to the apples to speed up the fermenting process. She had plans to serve the wine one night soon, and she wanted a potent brew. Let him try being nasty after a swig or two of this, she thought, smiling, as she stirred the bubbling potion.

If black moods were money, Chase Beaudine would have been a wealthy man. He was in another of his legendary foul tempers as he drove the Bronco home from what promised to be the most frustrating investigation of his career. He'd been concentrating full time on the serious cattle thefts ever since he'd put Bad Luck Jack in jail. Jack had been a nuisance more than anything else, but Chase was damn glad to have the man out of his hair. Only now that Chase was ready and waiting for them, the rustlers were lying low, as though they knew he'd intensified his hunt.

As he pulled the Bronco onto the rutted road that led to his cabin, the car's groaning springs summed up his state of mind and body perfectly. He was one big raw, aching nerve. Even the battle scar on his thigh was plaguing him. He hadn't slept in days, and his digestion was off, though he suspected those ailments had more to do with a certain tiny, red-headed houseguest than with cattle thieves.

If he didn't die of black moods, then Annie Wells was the next most likely candidate to put him in an early grave. To her credit, she'd been trying hard to stay out of his way. Maybe she couldn't help it that her whispery voice stroked his imagination and filled his head with vivid, X-rated daydreams. Maybe she couldn't help it that she was a soft, delectable, thoroughly frustrating female.

He'd made the mistake of unburdening himself about the rustlings one night after a couple beers too many. Annie had listened intently while he described how modern-day rustlers operated with moving vans and walkie-talkies, how they hit in the middle of the night and were gone without a trace.

"Did you ever try putting a radio beacon on a steer?" she'd suggested when he finished. "They did that in one of the western novels I read. Caught the rustler red-handed. He turned out to be the ranch's own foreman. Can you imagine?"

Chase patiently explained that rustlers were "high tech" these days. They had scanning equipment and detection devices.

"Well, don't let that discourage you," she'd counseled, her expression utterly sincere. "Machinery can't compete with the human spirit. The unconquerable soul, that's what Sister Maria Innocentia always called it. She used to say that if it weren't for perseverance, the snail wouldn't have made it to the ark."

Snail? Ark? Chase wanted to believe he'd heard her wrong. But no such luck. As it turned out, Annie had a proverb for every occasion, and Chase was to be the beneficiary of her storehouse of wisdom. Unfortunately one of her favorites was the Golden rule, which Chase loathed above all other proverbs. It brought back memories of his childhood, including the singsong voice of his third-grade teacher, who invariably recited it to him just before cracking his knuckles with a ruler.

He'd endured many such humiliations as a kid, both from his teachers and his parents, and he'd never forgotten their sting. Maybe his cocky attitude had provoked some of the punishment, but much of it was clearly abuse, meted out by alcoholic parents who hadn't the time or the patience to deal with their difficult offspring, and by teachers who had come to expect bad behavior from a kid with his background.

"Bad stock," a teacher had once whispered when Chase was summoned to the principal's office for fighting on the playground. "What do you expect of a Beaudine?"

But it wasn't grade-school nightmares on Chase's mind as he finally pulled the Bronco up in front of the cabin that night. It was rest for the wicked. He was dog-tired, ready for a hot shower and some sack time. He gathered up his equipment, grabbing his bullwhip as he piled out of the car.

A rich and spicy aroma greeted him as he shouldered open the cabin door and dropped his cargo on the table near the cot. "Doesn't smell like meat and potatoes to me," he said to Annie, who stood at the stove, hovering over a huge pot of something that was bubbling ferociously. She'd obviously been cooking up a storm.

"It's a version of an Indian dish called *fiambre*," she said, turning to him, a wooden spoon in her hand. "I thought we both needed a change, and I finally figured out how to make it with what you had here." Her hopeful expression implored him to overlook her slight breach of the rules. "Want to try some of my apple wine?"

With a flick of the spoon she indicated a glass of pale amber liquid sitting on the countertop. She'd either been cooking with it or sipping it, Chase decided, noting the sparkle in her eyes. Probably a little of both. She had pinned up her hair as though to restrain it, but without much success. There were loose straggles and tendrils flying every which way. And she'd gone back to wearing her own clothes— the cardigan sweater and blue jeans—which fit her a whole lot better than his clothes did, he had to admit.

"Sure," he said, too tired to argue. "Pour me a glass while I'm washing up."

Annie's Indian dish turned out to be a savory and delicious concoction, full of rice, chicken, and vege- tables. Chase wolfed it down hungrily, realizing only after he'd finished most of it that it had the flash- point of an atomic bomb. The cumulative effect was hotter than all the fires of hell combined, and it took him several glasses of apple wine to tamp down the blaze.

"What's wrong?" Annie asked as he pushed back from the table and pounded his chest. You don't like it?"

"No, it's great. I love food that burns a hole in my esophagus and turns the lining of my stomach to ash." He poured another glass of the wine and drank it down.

"Oh. Didn't I mention that it was hot?" Annie forked up a morsel of chicken, chewing it with intent concern. "Well, at least you seem to like the wine," she said. "I was afraid you might not. The nuns used to say it was an acquired taste."

Chase emptied what was left of the pitcher into his glass and finished it off. "Love the stuff. Got any more?"

"Be careful." She took a sip from her own glass and smiled at him. "It sneaks up on you."

Like the food, Chase thought, gradually becoming aware of a perfumy resonance as the fire in his throat cooled down. Annie went to get him another glass of wine, and as they sat across from each other, sipping slowly, Chase felt a welcome relaxation begin to steal through him. "Actually this isn't half-bad," he said, setting the glass down. "How do you make it?"

She began to describe the process, and Chase

settled back in his chair, kicking up his leg and resting a booted foot on his knee. The room was suffused with pink and gold light pouring in through the front windows, and he was absently aware of how beautiful it was, and how ethereal it made her look. Sun must be going down, he thought, fascinated with the way the rich light framed her hair, creating a halo effect.

Angel gone wild. The reference stole into his mind, but it didn't seem appropriate in her present state. She looked soft and reflective, an angel more intent on wisdom than wildness. Little did he know that the question about to drop out of her mouth would be anything but angelic.

"Have you ever been seduced?" she asked, regarding him almost pensively.

"Seduced? As in sexually?"

"Is there any other way?"

"Yeah, lots of ways. Why do you want to know?"

"Well—" Her brow knit, and she settled back in her chair with a faint sigh. "Because I can't imagine how she managed it."

Chase had to think about that one himself. Actually he had been seduced once, by a very ingenious girl in high school. She'd driven him nuts, flirting, and then acting as though she weren't the slightest bit interested when he took the bait. Their mating dance had gone on for weeks until he'd finally cornered her in the gymnasium. It had been one of the hottest experiences of his young life.

"How did she do it?" Annie asked again.

He picked up the glass of wine, watching the rich pink rays of sunlight penetrate its amber depths before he looked up and met her waiting gaze. "She let me think I was seducing her."

Five

The Appaloosa nickered softly as Chase adjusted the cinch on his saddle. He slapped the big horse gently on the flank, caught hold of the reins, and was about to swing himself into the saddle when he heard Annie calling his name.

"Chase!"

He turned to see her descending the front porch steps, holding his bullwhip. "I thought you might need this," she called out, hurrying toward the small corral where Chase kept Smoke and his two other horses, both mares.

She arrived breathless and seeming pleased with herself that she'd caught him. Chase took the whip from her and nodded his thanks, aware that her hair was all astray and her eyes misty. She looked as if she'd just rolled out of bed, which was probably true. She'd been asleep on the cot when he'd left the house a half hour earlier. He'd noticed then that the quilt had slipped off her, but he'd judiciously decided to leave it where it lay on the floor. He'd also noticed the way she slept—curled up like a kitten.

It was two days after she'd made him the *fiambre* dinner, and now, as she stood there, gazing up at him expectantly, he couldn't avoid noticing several other things about her, including the fact that she had nothing on under her unbuttoned cardigan sweater but the shift she wore night, day, and in the shower. "'Virtue is its own reward'?" he said, reading the words stitched into the thin fabric covering her breasts.

She glanced down. "Oh, yes, that. It means—"

"I know what it means."

She looked up and held his gaze for several seconds, something Chase wasn't used to having people do. Men and women alike usually flinched from his stare—or at least had the decency to look uneasy—and it almost gave him a chill when she didn't. She spoke at last, but typically, what she said wasn't what he'd expected to hear at that moment.

"Can I go with you today, Chase?" she asked. "Just this once." She indicated the roan mare in the corral behind them. "Fire and I are already friends, and I won't get in the way."

She'd asked to go with him almost every day, but Chase had refused categorically, for many reasons. The only thing that kept him from saying no immediately this time was his collie, Shadow. The dog had parked himself next to Annie, and he was whimpering softly, as if to say he was on Annie's side.

"Sorry, Red," Chase said. "I'm riding security on the McAffrey ranch today. If anything came up, I wouldn't know what to do with you."

Hardening himself against her crestfallen expression, Chase swung onto his horse, whistled for the dog, and started off. It wasn't until he reached the edge of the clearing that he realized Shadow wasn't trotting alongside him. He pulled the Appaloosa to a halt and twisted around, surprised to see the Border collie still sitting next to Annie. The two of them looked like a couple of characters in a Norman Rockwell sketch.

"Come on, boy!" Chase called over his shoulder, but Shadow didn't move. Chase tipped up his Stetson and glared at the two of them. "What are you doing to the dog?" he yelled to Annie.

She shrugged as though to say "Nothing."

Chase called the dog again, several times, but

Shadow remained statuelike. Baffled, Chase brought his horse around and started toward the troublesome pair, coming to a halt maybe twenty feet away from them.

"I think Shadow's trying to say we're a team," said Annie, patting the dog's head. "If you want one of us, you take us both."

"That's blackmail," Chase muttered, unable to keep the incredulity from his voice. He reached automatically for the thin strip of rawhide that secured the whip to the saddle horn—and then wondered what the hell he was doing. A man didn't crack the whip at Norman Rockwell characters. Not unless he was Simon Legree.

He stared at the two of them a long time, willing lightning to strike where it would do the most good. But the sky never even clouded over, and finally he conceded that Annie Wells probably had God on her side too. The woman didn't fight fair.

"Aw, the hell with it," he said abruptly. "Go on inside and get your clothes on. But if anything goes wrong on this trip, it's your butt in the sling, Missy."

A short time later they were riding out, just one big, happy family. Only now it reminded Chase of a full-fledged Norman Rockwell painting where Mom and the pooch were alight with secret pleasure, Dad looked disgruntled, and all three of them knew why. Even the horses seemed to be in on the joke.

Chase tried to convince himself he was doing the right thing in letting Annie come along, but it was no easy task. Finally he decided it might be worth the trouble of having her in tow if it kept her busy and got her mind off that seduction business she'd been preoccupied with lately. She'd been asking him leading questions about men and women and sex, never flirtatiously, more with the intent concentration of someone determined to learn.

But Chase needn't have worried about Annie at that moment. She was busy, indeed. She'd never been on a horse before, and Chase had given her only a few cursory instructions. He'd told her to sit the horse like a fork, her body being the handle, her legs the tines. With that in mind, she was doing her best to imitate a kitchen utensil, but it felt strange and awkward having such a huge thing moving beneath her. She felt like a salad fork on a big piece of steak.

At least she got the hang of the horse's gait quickly enough, and soon she was swaying comfortably in the saddle, aware of a sense of accomplishment as she enjoyed the scenery. The Wyoming foothills were vastly different from a tropical rain forest where the vegetation was lush and chokingly thick. Here, slender-limbed aspens, willows, and birches rustled gracefully in the same breezes that swept the verdant meadows and tousled the apple-green pasture grass. It was all so glorious and inspiring to the soul. *I could love it here,* she thought.

Even Shadow seemed energized by the bright, sunny day. He was as full of mischief as a puppy, chasing butterflies and racing around the horses, barking. Annie glanced at Chase occasionally for any sign that he might be loosening up a little too. But he remained silent and remote until Shadow made the mistake of sticking his nose in a prickly pear cactus and jumping back with a surprised yelp. Hearing Chase's low, husky laughter, Annie glanced at him, and their eyes connected for a moment.

Annie felt as though she'd been jolted by an open current of electricity as he held her gaze. The natural sensuality in his smile took her breath away, and without realizing she'd done it, she drew her horse to a stop, watching him and the Appaloosa pull away from her. With his dusty black Stetson tilted low and his buckskin vest stretched tight across his shoulders, he cut a powerful figure on the huge animal. Watching him made Annie feel desperately strange inside. Loose and warm. Meltingly warm.

Chase glanced over his shoulder. "Coming, Missy?"

Annie felt a tug in her stomach, as though he'd yanked a tether that was connected to her vital parts. She wasn't sure she liked him calling her Missy when he'd first done it. But she was beginning to like it now. Yes, indeed.

By the time they reached the east pasture of the McAffrey ranch, Chase was back to business, warning Annie to keep her horse under control, and ordering Shadow to stop his cavorting. "Longhorns can be unpredictable," he said, pointing out the herd that grazed the rolling grasslands that stretched before them. "We don't want to spook them and start a stampede."

As they rode just outside the fenced area, Annie noticed that Chase kept one hand casually resting on the wooden handle of his whip, much the way a gunslinger's hand might hover near his holster. Finally curiosity made her ask a question that had been at the back of her mind ever since she'd met him.

"Why do you use a bullwhip, Chase? It's such an unusual weapon."

"It gets the job done with less damage," he explained, smiling mysteriously. "For example, I can disarm a man without killing him . . . or undress a woman without touching her."

Annie stopped her horse again. She stared at him in astonishment, a fine trembling in her fingertips as they pulled the reins taut. "I don't believe you."

"About disarming a man?" He reined in his horse and turned to look at her. "Or undressing a woman?"

"That part—the woman." She'd actually seen him disarm a man in Costa Brava, so she couldn't question that.

"Want a demonstration?"

"No!"

But Chase was already pulling the coiled whip off the horn of his saddle and urging his horse across the path they'd just traveled toward an unfenced, flower-filled meadow. Annie followed him reluctantly, aware that he was putting some distance between them and the herd.

He flicked the whip out behind him as he rode,

letting the braided-leather thong trail on the ground like a loose rope. But the snakelike rawhide didn't sound like a rope as he suddenly swung it up in a powerful, fluid arc and cracked it in the air.

The whining snap electrified Annie. It was so sharp and riveting to the nerves, she wanted to gasp. Black lightning, she thought. He could claim the thing was harmless all he wanted, but it seemed downright deadly to her. At least she could be thankful for one thing. He wasn't demonstrating on her!

Just beyond Chase and the snorting Appaloosa, a patch of wild daisies swayed in the breeze, their delicate white petals fluttering. Annie watched, reluctantly fascinated as Chase drew the whip back again. Please let him put it away now, she thought. Instead, he swung the thong up in another stunning, recoiling arc of motion.

His second throw amazed her even more than the first one had. The whip reared back like a cobra about to strike, then flashed low to the ground, zinging toward its target. With surgical precision it snapped one of the daisies clean, severing the flower's stem at its base. Annie watched in mute wonderment as he swung off the horse and picked up the flower, turning back to her. His eyes were dark and sexy, charged with erotic undercurrents.

"You like flowers?" he asked.

She shook her head, an instinctive reaction that had nothing to do with whether or not she liked flowers. It just seemed the wisest response under the circumstances.

He walked to her anyway and offered her the daisy. "It'll look better in your hair than mine," he said.

Annie took it automatically, tucking it above her ear and mustering a smile. Anything to keep the man with the whip happy.

"Do you want to get down?" he asked. "Stretch your legs?"

She wasn't at all sure what she wanted to do, but somehow being on solid ground sounded reassuring. "You're very good with that thing," she said rather belatedly as she allowed him to help her off the horse. "The whip, I mean."

She swung her leg over the saddle and slid toward the ground, facing him, silently thrilling to the feel of his hands on her waist as he caught her and set her down. Their clothing brushed as he held her that way for a moment before releasing her. All she had to do was stand still, and she would be closer to him than she'd been all week! And exactly where she'd always wanted to be. *So stand still, Annie,* she told herself.

"My, it's warm today, isn't it?" she said, aware of the moisture at the back of her collar. Without glancing up, she inched out from between him and the horse, a hot spot if ever there was one. "I'm actually damp after all that riding."

He'd loaned her one of his old cotton shirts, shrunk from years of washing, and she was wearing it under her open cardigan sweater. She busied herself getting out of the sweater, tying it around her waist, and then fanning herself with her hand as she glanced up at him. "Don't you think it's warm?"

He regarded her silently. Beneath his tilted Stetson his eyes were smoky-black and faintly intrigued. Was that his getting-down-to-it look? she wondered, feeling herself flush and grow even warmer. Why in the world was she suddenly acting like a schoolgirl with a crush? Now of all times?

"You probably ought to be wearing a hat out here in all this direct sunshine," he said, taking off his Stetson and raking back his wavy black hair. "You're getting a burn, Missy."

He popped the Stetson on her head, and if it hadn't been for the volume of her hair, the hat would have dropped to her nose. Feeling a little silly, she adjusted it while he knelt to pick up the whip.

"This thing seems to be making you nervous," he said as he coiled the rawhide thong. "Maybe you ought to learn how to use it."

"No, thank you." She did not want to touch that whip. Annie had never been so sure of anything in her life. His prowess with the weapon had unnerved her, no doubt about it. But it was more than that. The fear she felt seemed almost instinctive, and she wouldn't have been surprised if it had something to do with the whip's physical similarity to the poisonous reptiles of the rain forest. She'd never got used to the coiled menace of a jungle snake, either on the forest floor or high in the trees.

"I think I'll take your suggestion and stretch my legs," she said, her voice softening to the hushed tone she'd used in the convent. "Here, you can have this back." She handed him the hat and turned away from his questioning gaze, walking deeper into the meadow.

"I could show you how to crack a whip in no time at all."

"No . . ."

He was silent a moment, and then his husky voice caught her, caressed her. "It's no good running away from things, Annie. They always catch up to you, one way or another."

"I'm not running," she said. "I'm walking."

Her heart was pounding with a strange and dizzying force as she made a pretense of being enraptured by the wildflowers that created a rainbowlike panorama in the meadow's green velvet carpet. "Aren't they lovely!" she exclaimed, heading for a patch of columbines that fanned out alongside the daisies.

"Annie."

He called her name in a way that made her freeze in the act of kneeling to look at flowers.

"What's wrong," he asked.

"Nothing . . ."

"Turn around then, talk to me."

His voice tugged at her irresistibly, that hot tether again, connected to her vitals. "Leave me alone," she implored softly. "I just want to pick some of these flowers."

"Annie . . . I'm not going to ask you again."

Her hand began to tremble as she stubbornly ignored him and knelt to pick the flower. And then she felt something stroke her back lightly. A delayed crack of sound jolted her upright, and when she glanced down, her sweater was gone from her waist. She whirled and saw him dangling the article from his fingertips, the whip handle clutched loosely in his right hand.

"Why did you do that?" she demanded.

"To get your attention." He threw her sweater over the saddle horn of the mare. "What is it you're afraid of, Annie? The whip? There's no need."

He looked like some kind of desperado with his black hair flying in the breeze and the black kerchief he wore tied loosely around his neck. Taking him in all at once, Annie found her eyes drawn to the way he was standing, one leg cocked and his faded blue jeans stretched tight across his hips.

"Of course there's need," she said, clutching a hand to her midriff, where the sweater had been tied. "Whips are dangerous. People get hurt."

"Not with this whip." His eyes brushed over her breasts, lingering there a moment. "I could undo every button of that shirt you're wearing, and you'd never feel a thing."

She stepped back, her throat constricting painfully. "That's insane. You wouldn't—"

"Easy does it now," he said, shaking the whip out. "I'm not going to hurt you. Just stand very still."

"No! Chase, no!" she cried as he drew the handle back.

"Annie! *Stand still!*"

"Oh, God!" She closed her eyes, terrified as he brought up his arm and the flash of black lightning cracked in the air high over her head. She began to tremble, a shock wave moving through her body like a thunderbolt. And then there was a rush of something that sounded like water roaring in her ears.

Just as she opened her eyes, he threw the whip again, aiming for her this time, and she felt a heat and a power beyond description as the thong coiled softly around her middle and yanked her forward. A scream locked in her throat.

"Easy does it, Annie. You're okay."

His voice echoed distantly, part of the thunder as she stumbled toward him, drawn by his muscular power on the whip, and by some other terrifying force that stormed through her like a roaring wind. The landscape blurred, and Chase's dark eyes penetrated her consciousness, the only thing she could see for a moment. She grabbed hold of the leather thong like a lifeline, pitching forward as he tugged at it.

"Don't fight the whip, Annie. You'll make it tighter."

By the time she reached him, she was shaking and half-drunk on the river of adrenaline gushing through her system. The whip loosened, slithering to the ground, and she would have slithered with it, if he hadn't caught her.

"Here—I've got you," he said, taking her into his arms. "Grab hold of me."

She clung to him weakly, only vaguely aware of taut muscles and male power, and of the long line of his body as she pressed herself up against him. Such heat, she thought, soaking up the warmth he gave off. Such blessed strength. She knew she ought to be angry, furious even, that he had so deliberately frightened her, but she didn't have the energy for it. She'd been sapped of every ounce of strength. All that was left was a quaking need to be held, to be enveloped by his sheltering arms.

Gradually she became aware of the way she'd locked herself to him, of his heartbeat and his breathing, of his stony thigh muscles and hipbones. But most of all she reveled in the way his arms encompassed her, one bracing her shoulders, the other locked firmly around her waist. Within moments the power of his hold had matched, then begun to subdue, the awesome, seemingly destructive power inside her.

"See there," he said, his hand cradling her head against his chest as he caressed her hair. "You're okay, Missy. You didn't feel a thing, did you?"

"I don't like whips," she said, a sob in her voice.

"So I gather. Sorry if I frightened you."

"Sorry?" She looked up at him, wishing fervently that she could summon some anger, just enough to swear at him—a couple of soul-satisfying four-letter words would do. Sister Maria Innocentia wouldn't have liked it, but she was thousands of miles away. And Chase wasn't. No, he most certainly wasn't. Lord, the feel of him so close and sexy was about to do Annie in. He was too much for a woman in her weakened condition. His eyes were as black as carbon. And his body was so wonderfully hard to the touch. And so damn big. There, she had sworn at him.

"I wanted you to see there was nothing to be afraid of," he explained. "But you wouldn't hold still long enough. I thought a little demonstration would be the quickest way to ease your mind."

She shook her head. "Next time don't be so all-fired quick about easing my mind, thank you."

He seemed amused as he studied her expression. "What are you saying, girl? That I rushed you? If I remember correctly, you seemed disappointed the last time I wanted to slow things down."

The "last time" was their very first encounter, Annie realized, probably the closest they had ever come to actually making love. And maybe ever would. He'd told her he wanted to make love to her that day. He'd said those exact words, and she would never forget the rough thrill of his voice, or the heat of his mouth on hers.

"Well then, maybe you ought to just go ahead"—her voice caught, trembling—"and rush me."

His eyes darkened, hotly aware of what she meant. "Don't tempt me, Miss Annie," he warned, his fingers biting into the flesh of her hip. "You might not like what you get."

"I'll like it," she said. "I promise."

Seconds flashed by, each one of them a burning eternity as he stared down at her. He curved his hand to her throat, his fingers splaying out, his thumb stroking her jawline. "I wonder if you know what you're asking for," he whispered harshly, tipping up her chin.

Annie made a sound as he bent to kiss her. But it wasn't a moan, or even a sigh. The inaudible whimper came straight from her soul, and it was sweet and softly anguished.

"I'll like it," she whispered as his lips touched hers. "I promise . . ."

His breath hissed out, and his arms contracted around her, bringing their bodies together. Annie felt the crush of him all at once, and it was a wonderful thing. She wanted to touch him, to tangle her fingers in his hair and kiss him back. But she couldn't move. There was something sparkling hot and terribly erotic trembling through her, and it made her ache for the rapture of his hard, hard love.

He deepened the kiss, turning it into something miraculous. Annie was clinging to him mindlessly when suddenly he broke away, his breath hot on her parted lips. An instant later the same hot, harsh breath was near her ear. "Annie, listen," he said. "Do you hear it? Horses . . . there's someone coming."

Horses? Why did he want her to listen to horses? All she wanted was to be closer to him. She wanted to drop to the ground and rip off their clothes and make love. Right then and there.

"Annie, do as I say, and don't ask questions." He held her back, his abruptness breaking through her euphoria. "Get Fire and take cover in the trees. Hear me? Do it! Quickly!"

She reacted automatically, stumbling away from him, reaching for the horse's reins. But as she was leading Fire around, she stopped cold. She didn't care if it was the Four Horsemen of the Apocalypse riding down on them. There was something she had to know. "Chase?" she said, catching him as he was scooping up his Stetson from the ground. "Could you have done it? Could you have undressed me with that whip?"

He swung the hat onto his head and tapped it

down, his dark eyes twinkling. "I'm good, but I'm not that good."

Moments later, hidden behind a stand of huge blue oaks, Annie watched as three men rode up, their mounts stomping and blowing from the run. The lead rider, a heavyset man with a mustache, gave Chase the grim details of another cattle theft. Annie was able to pick up from the conversation that he was the foreman of the McAffrey ranch.

"They hit the north pasture," the foreman said. "Looks like it happened some time last night."

Chase asked a few cursory questions, then told the men he'd meet them up at the north pasture. "My horse picked up a rock," he explained. "I'll be along in a minute."

As the men rode off, Annie emerged from the trees, leading Fire. She could see by Chase's pensive expression that he was preoccupied with this latest assault on the ranchers.

"Go on back to cabin," he told her, helping her onto the horse. "Fire knows the way. Take the dog with you, and stay there until I get back."

Once she was mounted, Annie took hold of the reins with unsteady hands. "When will that be?"

"When I get the sons of bitches responsible. They're starting to make me look bad."

"Maybe I could help you?" she suggested. "I have a feeling I'd be pretty good at tracking down bad guys."

"Annie, git," he said gruffly, giving her horse a slap. "If I'd been paying attention to what I was supposed to be doing, instead of to you, I might have had the rustlers by now."

Annie reined her horse around and started off, uneasiness weighing heavily on her mind. Though she knew bounty hunting was what Chase did for a living, she didn't much like the idea at the moment. What if he got hurt? Or was gone for days, weeks? She also regretted the abrupt way they'd been interrupted when they were making such progress. And beyond that, she was wondering what she was going to do with herself while he was gone.

She reached up absently and touched the flower she'd tucked in her hair—the daisy he'd picked for her with his whip. It seemed a miracle it had stayed in place through all the commotion. A thoughtful smile crossed her lips as she drew the flower out of her hair and studied it. The smile deepened as an idea took hold. She knew exactly what she wanted to do when she got back to the cabin. She just didn't know if she dared.

Six

"I'm going to do it," Annie said under her breath. She drew her forefinger down the dusty windowpane, leaving a streak of grime that made the trees outside Chase's cabin look as if they'd been struck down by biblical blight and pestilence. Even the dazzling morning sunshine, breaking over the hills, was shrouded in brown haze.

"I have to do it," she said, turning away from the window to survey her dismal surroundings. "This place is more depressing than medieval catacombs."

She'd been pacing the cabin's small living area, staring at bare walls and filthy windows until she couldn't stand it any longer. Chase had been gone for the last two days, and during that time she'd tried to talk herself out of the crazy idea that had taken up residence in her brain, but she couldn't hold out any longer.

The dog began to bark as she pulled the car keys off a hook near the door. "I'm sorry, Shadow," she said. "I can't take you with me, boy." *I shouldn't even be going myself.*

It didn't occur to her until she was climbing into the Bronco that she couldn't go anywhere looking as she did. Chase had been adamant about not wanting anyone to know he had a woman at his place, and even though he hadn't explained why, she didn't want to do anything, even inadvertently, that might cause him any more problems.

Moments later, after having made some last-minute alterations to her appearance, Annie was back in the driver's seat of the Bronco, turning the key in the ignition. The gears ground painfully as she shifted into reverse and pulled the car back. It had been a while since she'd driven, but luckily, she'd learned on a stick shift—in this case, a rusted-out military jeep that had been abandoned near the convent and repaired by the nuns themselves.

Once Annie had the Bronco on the road headed toward town, she glanced at her reflection in the rearview mirror. She'd tucked her hair up into a duckbilled John Deere cap she'd found in a closet and she'd borrowed a huge old army fatigue jacket, which easily concealed her breasts. She'd also smeared some fireplace soot over her chin and jaw-line in an attempt to disguise herself. It looked more like dirt than a beard, but she doubted anyone would automatically take her for a woman. More likely they'd think she was an unkempt young drifter looking for work on one of the oil rigs south of town—at least that was what she hoped.

It didn't take her long to get accustomed to the Bronco, and once she'd left the winding curves of the foothills for the white-gold grass of the plains, she was rolling right along on a stretch of highway that seemed endless and surreal. The road opened up on all sides, creating a pale, shimmering panorama that reflected sunlight like a mirrored pond.

The effect was strangely hypnotic, and Annie was slipping into a near-trancelike state when a sudden burst of static jarred her awake. It sounded like a radio caught between stations. "Road Hog?" a male voice called, cutting through the fuzziness. "You out there, buddy? Pick up if you are."

The noise seemed to be coming from the speaker of a radiolike apparatus on the console. Annie noticed a microphone and lifted it from its cradle, pressing the red button tentatively. "Are you calling me?" she asked.

"No, I sure wasn't, sweetheart," the male voice drawled thickly. "But you'll do. I'm Hopalong. What's your handle?"

"My handle? What does that mean?"

There was a snort of laughter on the other end. "Lady, where you been the last century? A convent?"

She nodded, then remembered she had to speak. "Yes, I was in a convent. How did you know?"

"I'll be damned!" He chuckled. "What kind of rig you drivin'? And how fast?"

Annie wasn't sure she ought to reveal the name of her "rig," but she glanced at the speedometer, and immediately lightened her foot as she read off the miles per hour.

"Eighty-five?" He let out a sharp whistle. "I got just the handle for you, sweetheart—the Flying Nun."

Whatever he said after that was drowned out in a burst of static, and the whole episode left Annie slightly perplexed but smiling. The Flying Nun? She rather liked the sound of that. Too bad she couldn't tell Chase.

Painted Pony came into view as she rounded a curve a short time later. The drowsy little cow town, stretched out in the valley below, was shaped like a shoehorn, and the glittering river that defined its northern border was lined by graceful willows and white birches. Golden sagebrush plains were the backdrop to it all, sweeping upward into hills so inky black, Annie couldn't make out their details even in the sunlight. Charmed by the vision, she told herself that the valley's beauty must be a sign that she was right in making the trip.

She avoided parking on the main street, deciding instead to hide the Bronco away in an alley one block down. The post office appeared deserted as she walked toward the city center, as did *The Painted Pony Express-Gazette* newspaper, and the crumbling stucco savings-and-loan building. The heat and still air had a heaviness to it that made Annie think of the afternoon *siestas* that were a way of life in Costa Brava.

Further investigation turned up plenty of activity inside some of the other establishments. The men's favorite haunts seemed to be the barber shop and Prairie Oyster Tavern, and a group of women were congregated across the street at the beauty parlor.

Prairie oyster, Annie mused, as she began her search for a dry-goods store. Wasn't that the local delicacy that Chase had mentioned? Too bad she wasn't going to have time to sample some. A half hour later she was on her way out of the town's general store with two sacks full of merchandise. She'd spent nearly every cent of the money she'd been hoarding, but she was thrilled with the ready-made yellow curtains and seat cushions she'd found. She'd also purchased some woven rugs for the cabin floor, a starter set of hand-painted stoneware dishes in vibrant colors, and a large vase to hold wildflowers.

Hoping it was true, she told herself that once Chase had seen what she'd done, he would understand and appreciate her efforts. He'd been living in that tomb of a cabin so long, he didn't realize how depressing it was. Someone had to put a touch of color in his life. Someone had to show him how things could be, given a favorable outlook and a little inspiration.

Her last stop was the drugstore. Chase hadn't considered her personal needs when he'd gone shopping for supplies, not that she would have expected him to. She didn't suppose most men thought about such things, although she had no way of actually knowing. Her own father had been so distracted by his research on tropical diseases, he'd gone off to investigate a new strain of malaria while her mother was giving birth to her.

Of course, Sarah Wells had been a doctor, too, and perfectly capable of handling the situation from a medical standpoint. But Annie had always wondered how her mother had survived it—and all of the other hardships—emotionally. The jungle was an awesome place, both beautiful and terrible. It was at once irresistibly seductive to the senses and perversely inhospitable to human life.

But it wasn't the jungle that had killed her parents, Annie reminded herself, as she hesitated in one of the drugstore aisles, gazing at the vast array of modern medicines. It wasn't nature, it was men. The population centers of Costa Brava were a hotbed of civil war and insurrection that had finally invaded even the jungle. Her parents' outpost had been stormed by guerrillas demanding medical help, and when her parents had refused to abandon the *indigenas*, their Indian patients, they'd been shot. It was only through the help of the Indians that Annie had escaped and taken refuge in the convent.

She still felt anguish about the terrible meaninglessness of it all, the wanton disregard for human life. She had adored both her parents, and missed them terribly, even now. If they'd neglected her at times, it was a benign neglect, and one she had come to understand eventually. They felt called to a higher mission—saving lives, eradicating disease. . . .

"Oh, excuse me!" said Annie, stumbling forward as a large man jostled past her in his impatience to get to the pharmacist's counter. The impact jarred Annie out of her reflections and brought her back to the reason she'd come to the drugstore. She found the feminine-hygiene section in the next aisle, but it wasn't until she'd begun to pick out what she needed that she became aware of her predicament. She was dressed up like a young tough. What were they going to say when she arrived at the checkout counter with shampoo, facial soap, and a box of sanitary napkins?

Since she didn't have any immediate need for the napkins, she went on to the other items. But as she was pondering the enormous selection of shampoos, she was distracted by a man's hushed voice. It drifted to her from over her right shoulder.

"Got me some plumbing problems, if you know what I mean," he whispered. "Need a little—"

"Roto-rooting?" a second man suggested, chuckling.

Annie glanced around, curious, and saw the man who'd bumped her conferring with a pharmacist, who happened to be recommending a huge bottle of chalky blue liquid. There was something familiar about the customer's profile, but Annie was more interested in the laxative he was considering. If he drank that stuff, she thought, he wouldn't have any plumbing left.

The man declined as though he'd heard Annie's silent warning. And then he stopped down the aisle from her to check out a display of antacids. Annie found herself watching him out of the corner of her eye. He looked to be around thirty-five, a little young to be having digestive problems.

"Raw fruits and vegetables might be helpful," she suggested, smiling as he turned to her. His look of wary surprise made her hesitate.

"Helpful for what?"

"Plumbing," she said quietly, going with his choice of words. "Mangoes in particular are good for peristaltic action and lubricating the alimentary system. And if you're looking for a natural purgative, try cabbage juice, or rhubarb roots." She indicated the display with a nod of her head. "All much better for you than that stuff, which kills friendly bacteria, washes out vitamins, plugs up intestinal walls, and—"

"Hold it!" He held up his hands as though overwhelmed. "Mangoes? Rhubarb roots?"

Annie gave him a reassuring nod. "Even tree bark will do. As far as North American trees go, I think senna's the best."

He regarded her with a furrowed brow, as though trying to make sense of both the advice and the adviser. "Let me get something straight," he said, scrutinizing her appearance. "You're a girl, right?"

Annie's heart sank as she glanced down at herself.

She'd completely forgotten how she was dressed. Better not to bluff, she decided. "Could this be our secret?" she said. "I'd just as soon it didn't get around."

His expression took on a life all of its own, sliding from confusion to disbelief to incredulity. Somewhere in the midst of all that activity, Annie realized where she'd seen him before. He was the foreman from the McAffrey ranch. He and his two men had reported the cattle theft the day she and Chase were out riding the range. Luckily none of the men had seen her.

"Could I give you a tip?" he said.

"Please. I gave you one."

"If you're trying to pass for a guy around here, lose the duckbill, get yourself a cowboy hat, some boots, and some chewin' tobacco. Then, if anybody talks to you, just nod and spit."

"Oh, thank you," Annie said.

"Not a problem." He tipped his Stetson, picked up a bottle of the chalky blue stuff, and went to the register.

Annie turned back to the shelves and selected a shampoo that promised to turn her hair into silken splendor. Nod and spit. She would have to remember that.

"It's a miracle," Annie said softly, gazing at the transformation that had taken place in Chase's cabin in just a few hours' time. Now it really was the cozy, rustic setting she'd fantasized—and the home she'd never had. Once she'd got started, she'd cleaned with a vengeance, even to the point of pulling everything out of the cupboards and scrubbing their insides. She'd found all manner of strange things in the cabinets and drawers, including Chase's marine dog tags, Wanted posters, an unsprung mousetrap, and a dead lizard. And dust, of course. Dust old enough to be prehistoric, she imagined.

IF YOU LOVE ROMANCE... THEN YOU'RE READY TO BE "LOVESWEPT"!

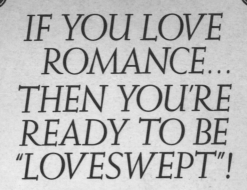

Mail this heart today! (see inside)

**LOVESWEPT INVITES YOU
TO OPEN YOUR HEART
TO LOVE
AND WE'LL SEND YOU
6 BOOKS TO EXAMINE —
RISK-FREE, A FREE EXCLUSIVE
ROMANCE NOVEL
AND MUCH MORE**

OPEN YOUR HEART TO LOVE...
YOU'LL BE LOVESWEPT WITH THIS OFFER!

HERE'S WHAT YOU GET:

1. **RISK-FREE!** SIX NEW LOVESWEPT NOVELS! Preview 6 beautiful stories filled with passion, romance, laughter and tears . . . exciting romances to stir the excitement of falling in love . . . again and again.

2. **FREE!** AN EXCLUSIVE ROMANCE NOVEL! You'll receive *Larger Than Life* by the best-selling author Kay Hooper ABSOLUTELY FREE. You won't find it in bookstores anywhere. Instead, it's reserved for you as our way of saying "thank you."

3. **SAVE!** MONEY-SAVING HOME DELIVERY! Join the Loveswept at-home reader service and we'll send you 6 new novels each month. You always get 15 days to preview them before you decide whether to keep it. Each book is yours for only $2.25 — a savings of 54¢ per book.

4. **BEAT THE CROWDS!** You'll always receive your Loveswept books before they are available in bookstores. You'll be the first to thrill to these exciting new stories.

BE LOVESWEPT TODAY — JUST COMPLETE, DETACH AND MAIL YOUR RISK-FREE ORDER CARD.

She'd also found a battered picture of Chase, Johnny Starhawk, and Geoff Dias in their mercenary days. The three men had been celebrating in a bar somewhere, probably a foreign port, grinning at the camera and hoisting their drinks. They'd looked young and reckless and momentarily jubilant in their military fatigues, cropped hair, and aviator sunglasses.

Annie had felt caught in a time warp as she studied the picture. It wrenched her back to the very first time she'd set eyes on Chase, triggering flashbacks of the young, brash hero who'd saved her life. The lump that formed in her throat expanded painfully as she turned the picture over and saw Chase's note scrawled on the back. "First Mission—Teheran, Iran—ten American prisoners recovered," he'd written. "We kicked butt!"

She'd had to remind herself forcefully to put the picture away and finish her project, but even then the images had lingered, stirring a sadness that was oddly sweet.

It wasn't until the housecleaning purge was over and she'd rested for a while that she had fully recovered her momentum. Reinspired, she'd hung the curtains and attached the seat cushions to the kitchen chairs. She'd also distributed the woven rugs about the freshly waxed living-room floor like lily pads on a mirrored pond. And then she'd filled the vase, the blue coffeepot, and a couple of glasses with wildflowers. The effect was dazzling. If a cabin had a face, this one was smiling.

The only room she hadn't touched was his bedroom. She'd already courted as much disaster as she dared. But she had been tempted. Even now, having put a spicy Spanish soup bubbling on the stove in the hope that Chase might be back in time for dinner, she was marshaling arguments against investigating that dark sanctuary off the main room.

"Charity, chastity, piety, *and* privacy," she reminded herself, invoking four of the most basic tenets of the cloister. She probably hadn't scored many points where the first three were concerned, but at least she could show a little respect for the last one.

An hour later, after finishing the soup herself and doing the dishes, Annie still had the entire evening ahead of her. As she lingered at the kitchen table, sipping some of her homemade wine, the darkened bedroom took on an almost irresistible allure. With each guilty glance in its direction, her show of respect for Chase's privacy was losing ground, until finally it turned into a moral tug-of-war, with curiosity yanking the rope and dragging respect over the line.

Just a peek, she told herself. I'll stand in the doorway.

Shadow began to bark as Annie approached the room, which had the effect of making her all the more curious. From the door's threshold things looked normal enough. There was the usual clutter of clothes and personal effects, plus a brass bed that didn't look much sturdier than the cot she slept on. There was even an old western saddle propped on a sawhorse in the corner. But nothing secret or sinister, other than the fact that there were no windows, which did seem a little odd.

She was turning away when a glint of metal caught her eye, drawing her attention to the far corner of the dark room. It wasn't perpendicular like a normal corner, and there was something odd about its rough, uneven surface. That section of the wall appeared to be solid rock, she realized. She had noticed from the outside that the western corner of the cabin was built up against a granite bluff, but it had never occurred to her that it might be built into the hill.

She could just make out a door that looked as though it might lead to some sort of underground storm cellar. The glint of metal that had caught her eye must have come from its padlock. Fascinated, she stepped into the room. Shadow, who'd been whimpering the entire time, immediately erupted into barking.

"Hush, Shadow," she said. "I only want to take a look."

She tried the padlock and was startled when it fell open in her hands. Either the rust had corroded its parts, or it hadn't been locked. Whatever the reason, it seemed an invitation to investigate. Shadow's barking became deafening as Annie tugged and heaved, forcing the heavy door open. Even if the dog's reaction hadn't frightened her, the musty gloom she encountered beyond the doorway would have. The tunnel, if that's what it was, looked pitch-black and impenetrable.

She crouched to quiet Shadow as she tried to decide what to do. Common sense told her to end her investigation right there, and the dog seemed to agree. But as her eyes began to adjust to the darkness and she was able to discern that it was a deep, rock-ribbed passageway, she knew she had to find out where it led.

A moment later, using matches she'd found by the fireplace, she made her way through what seemed like a natural corridor into a larger limestone cavern. There were no signs of recent use or anything to indicate the cavern's purpose, and Annie had decided to turn back when she noticed another tunnel branching off at a 45-degree angle.

This time she resisted temptation. "Let's go back," she told Shadow. The dog's nervous whine sharpened the eerie stillness. As Annie turned around, she noticed her match had burned down perilously low. Its heat seared her skin as she fumbled with the matchbox, trying to get it open. "Ouch!" she cried as the pain flared. The box tumbled out of her grip, and the match dropped with it, pitching the cavern into inky blackness.

Panic gripped her as she knelt down, searching blindly for the matches with her hands. The earth was icy cold and damp beneath her fingers, and she had the horrible feeling she was going to touch something alive, something slimy. "Shadow?" she called out, unable to find the matchbox. "Come here, boy." The dog could guide them both back.

"Shadow? Where are you?" Annie groped the darkness with her hands. Something was wrong. Terribly wrong. Where was the dog? It was too quiet, and the dank smell of moldering earth was suffocating.

"Shadow!" She could hear his bark, but it sounded tinny and distant. As she rose and stumbled toward the sound of it, she felt the clay give way beneath her feet. The crumbling earth pitched her forward into nothingness. Flailing the air, she stepped into a terrifying void and plummeted downward like a rock. "Chase!" she screamed, twisting, falling. . . .

Chase swore, jerked his shotgun from its leather scabbard, jammed the butt up against his shoulder, and pumped out four rounds in quick succession. He barely felt the powerful weapon's recoil as it kicked through taut muscle and braced bone. As the last shell hit home, he exhaled, breathing out tension and frustration in equal measure. He'd blown all four empty beer cans to hell and gone. He felt a little better. But not much.

Crying shame it hadn't been a cattle rustler in his sights, he thought, reining in his horse as he shoved the shotgun back into the scabbard. He'd been three days on the trail without a sign of the slippery bastards. Whoever they were, they'd pulled off another vanishing act with a hundred head of cattle. "Rustlers, hell," he muttered. "They're magicians."

He spurred his horse toward the hills, and the big Appaloosa snorted and reared, bolting into a gallop. Chase leaned into the wind, letting the horse have his head and savoring the smooth jolts of motion that rocked through his body. The animal probably needed the release of pent-up energy as much as he did, and there was damn little Chase enjoyed more than the powerful, fluid surge of a horse beneath him.

The pounding ride relaxed him, but despite his

efforts to lose himself in it, to find temporary oblivion, his mind was riveted on his destination. He couldn't rein in his thoughts any more than he could have reined in the snorting animal beneath him. They raced on ahead, Chase imagining the cabin he was headed for, and the woman waiting inside. He hadn't been able to keep his mind off her the entire trip, wondering if she'd still be there after all this time. And how he would feel if she wasn't.

She'd tumbled into his life in such a lunatic way, he half expected her to make just as quick and unpredictable an exit. Imagining her gone should have filled him with profound relief, but now that he was headed back, there was a kind of anticipation building in him . . . a desire, almost, to see her again.

That kind of notion was dangerous, he knew, but it seemed that the harder he tried to hold his feelings for her down, the more they sprang back, resilient as a willow branch, like her. Crazy thoughts of her had been buzzing around in his head all morning, images he couldn't extinguish . . . of her unruly red hair and that strange little bend in the bridge of her nose. For some unfathomable reason he'd been taken with the idea of kissing her there, touching his lips gently to that tiny aberration in her fine-boned features.

But the most vivid, torturous image was of her dripping wet in his hallway. That one had nearly destroyed him, cluttering up his head night after night. He was still aching inside, thinking about taking that transparent shift off her, about touching her damp skin and catching the soft swing of her breasts in his hands.

Chase groaned as the sheer pleasure of it hit him. His thighs locked tight around Smoke's quivering girth, spurring the horse on. Just one time he wanted to go all the way with Annie Wells. No fainting spells, no warning signals, no abrupt exits. Nothing to stop him! He wanted to hold her and love her and be as deep as he could get inside her. *Was that too much for a desperate man to ask?* Just once to rock in the fertile cradle of her hips, bucking like a crazed stallion, spilling his seed into her again and again until he was drained dry.

He reined in abruptly, pulling the horse to a shuddering stop as the graphic force of his thoughts struck home. Dust flew as Smoke bucked and danced, impatient to be set free again, but Chase held the reins taut. "If there's a God in heaven," he said under his breath, "if there's *any* mercy in this universe at all, Annie Wells will be gone when I get home."

The sun was peeking over the hilltops as Chase approached the clearing where his tiny cabin was nestled. He couldn't see any signs of life inside as he neared, but it was possible she wasn't up yet. It was still early.

Or had his prayers been answered?

The cabin door flew open, and Shadow bounded out as Chase dismounted his horse. He bent to greet the excited animal, trying to soothe him as he looked at the open doorway for Annie. There was still no sign of her, which was beginning to puzzle him. After he'd calmed the frantic dog a little, he rose to unfasten the cinch and pull the saddle off Smoke's back. He would corral the horse and feed and water him later. Right now he wanted to get inside and check things out.

"Ease up, Shadow," he said, as the dog's cries became piercingly sharp. "I'm going as fast as I can." He threw the saddle over the porch railing and then removed the bridle, letting it lie where it dropped to the ground as he bounded up the steps and into the house.

"What in hell?" He stopped dead inside the doorway, staring at the flowers and rugs and curtains . . . at a floor so shiny it made him want to shade his eyes. A cold kind of anger surged through him as he realized what she'd done. She'd turned his place into a goddam funeral parlor. "Annie?" he called out, turning to Shadow. "Where is that woman?"

The dog headed for the bedroom door, whining as

he turned back to Chase. Chase hesitated, a laser of fear nailing him to the floor. And then he followed the pleading animal. The open vault door was the first thing he saw as he entered the bedroom. "Oh, God, no," he muttered, his heart thudding painfully.

Seven

"Annie!" Chase shouted her name as he cut through the tunnel's gloom with the high beam of his flashlight. His own voice echoed thunderously, blocking out everything but the sound of Shadow's frantic barking.

The tunnel's acrid air burned Chase's nostrils with every breath he took, sharpening the urgency he felt. The cavern looked empty as he reached it and swept the flashlight beam around its circumference. But as the beam hit the cavern floor, he saw what had happened. The broken clods of dirt at the edge of the open pit confirmed his worst fears. She'd fallen in.

Chase's heart slammed against the wall of his chest. "Oh, God, Annie, no—" he said harshly.

Shadow went crazy as Chase approached the edge of the pit, and it was all he could do to prevent the dog from leaping in. The flashlight beam flickered wildly as he tried to direct it into the murky depths of a deadfall that was over twenty feet deep.

A soft moan of sound caught Chase's attention. He began a search for the source, and as the light finally illuminated Annie's slumped body, he dropped to his knees in relief. She was huddled in a corner of the pit, her arms hanging limp at her sides, her knees drawn up tight.

"Annie? Are you all right?"

She stirred slightly, as though summoning the energy to move. "Chase?" she said, lifting her head. When she looked up at him, her face was as pathetically dirt-smudged as the day she'd tumbled down the hill and landed at his feet.

"Listen to me, Annie. Are you hurt?"

Tears sprang to her eyes as she tried to speak. "No," she said in a hoarse, broken voice. "Nothing fractured, I don't think—just cuts and bruises. Oh, Chase, where have you been? I was afraid you weren't coming back."

Chase's heart felt as though it were going to twist out of his chest. He couldn't even answer her, he was so shaken. He'd had a moment of near panic thinking she was dead or badly hurt. Now all he wanted to do was get her out of the pit.

Moments later he had her cradled in one arm and was climbing up a rope ladder he'd secured with metal spikes. When he reached the bedroom, he settled her on his bed and sat next to her, brushing hair from her face, drying her tears with his fingers. A tenderness flowed through him that might have been the most powerful thing he'd ever felt. He was so damn grateful she was okay.

"I seem to have a talent for falling on my head, don't I?" she asked after a moment, her blue eyes even more vibrant against her smudged, tear-streaked skin.

"But you bounce good," he said, trying not to smile.

She smiled for both of them, ruefully. "Where does that man-eating tunnel go? And what is it for?"

"It was there when I bought the place. According to local legend, this cabin was once a hideout for a gang of horse thieves. The tunnel was their escape route if things got tight, and the pit took care of anyone who tried to follow them. Pretty good snare, huh?"

He found himself wanting to smooth her hair again, and say things to her that he'd never even thought about saying to a woman before. Silly, romantic things that might have worked for matinee idols in the movies but would have sounded awkward and foolish coming from Chase Beaudine.

"Do you hate what I did?" she asked suddenly.

"What you did?" She looked so expectant, Chase knew she couldn't possibly mean falling into the pit.

"The house, the way I fixed it up? Do you hate it?"

"No . . ." He loathed it—flowers and frilly curtains were probably the two things Chase hated most after cattle rustlers. But now didn't seem the time to tell her.

She caught hold of his hand, squeezing it with surprising strength. "You mean you like it?" Her voice was soft, hushed, confessional. "Really?"

"I didn't say that."

"But you don't hate it. You said you didn't hate it."

He nodded reluctantly, and sat back as she pushed herself to a sitting position, wincing and making little noises of distress at the apparent twinges of her body. "What are you doing now?" he asked, not bothering to hide his confusion, or his fraying patience.

She didn't answer immediately, apparently concentrating all her energy on the struggle to get around him and off the bed. "Come with me," she said when she'd finally reached her feet.

"Where?"

"I want to show you something."

He got up with the groan of a man who'd been on horseback too long, pulled off his leather vest, tossed it on the bed, and followed her, wondering what in hell was coming next. By the time he reached the kitchen, she was standing there with every one of the kitchen cabinets thrown open, looking like a hostess on one of those TV quiz shows.

"I bought us some dishes, Chase. Look." She reached into the cabinet, pulled a dish off the stack, and held it up for him to see. "They're glaze-baked and hand-painted. Aren't they beautiful?"

"Dishes? For us?" As Chase repeated the words, certain disturbing possibilities began to dawn on him. "Where did you get dishes, Annie? And all the rest of this stuff? You must have gone into town."

She returned the dish to the stack with exceeding care. "Only a quick trip."

Chase could feel his disbelief beginning to heat around the edges. "How'd you get there? Oh, hell! Not my Bronco?"

She looked up at him, guilty as charged, but apparently unwilling to accept the condemnation in his tone. "Well, yes . . . I couldn't very well walk."

"What were you thinking about, woman?"

"No one knew who I was. I disguised myself as a man."

"Oh, great," Chase said, trying to picture that spectacle in his mind. "A redheaded female cross-dresser driving my Bronco. That must have been quite an eyeful for the townsfolk."

She drew in a breath as though losing patience. "I hid the car in an alley. No one saw me driving it."

Chase swung around, growing more incredulous with every passing moment as he took in what she'd done to his home and hearth. Not to mention his life these last days. She was a human wrecking ball, shattering everything he thought was important, breaking down the walls of his fortress. "I told you not to mess with this house, didn't I? I told you not to mess with my things. What in hell did you think you were doing?"

"I only wanted to brighten it up a little. I thought once you'd seen it, you'd like it—"

"Like it?" He turned on her. "Don't you know you can't just traipse into people's houses and rearrange their lives? Dammit to hell, woman, you had no right."

She began to shut the cabinet doors, slowly at first, and then more quickly. When she turned around, tears were sparkling in her eyes. "I worked all day and night fixing this place up, and you don't appreciate anything I've done, do you? *Do you?*"

Her soft, hurt voice tugged at him, but he shook his head, refusing to be drawn into any more of her emotional traps. He was getting angry again, and dammit, he liked the feeling. It was a helluva lot better than the fear she'd struck in his heart when he'd thought she was dead. Or those stupid romantic notions he'd had in the bedroom.

"Appreciate it?" he said slowly, trying to track her thinking. "You steal my car, drive into town in drag, stink up my place with flowers so I don't even recognize it. Then you nose around in my bedroom, poking into places you have no business, and wind up nearly killing yourself. Call me an insensitive beast, but no—I don't appreciate that."

Annie tried to quiet the emotional tumult rising inside her. He did have a point, after all. She had done all the things he accused her of. She'd even expected him to be angry. What she hadn't expected were those moments of tenderness after he rescued her from the pit, that catch of emotion in his voice when he'd asked her if she was all right. If he hadn't been so concerned about her, so unaccountably gentle with her, then maybe it wouldn't hurt so much now that he hated everything she'd done. But it did hurt. God, it hurt.

"What you really want is to be rid of me, isn't it?" she said, turning away from him. The tears burning her eyes made her feel as foolish and inept as he obviously thought she was.

"Rid of you? That's putting it mildly, Missy. If I could toss you out of here on your fanny this minute, I'd do it without blinking."

"Well, then, why don't you?"

"Because you've got a piece of paper that says you're my wife, that's why. It's the slickest piece of emotional blackmail I've ever come up against."

She caught her breath, anger sharpening the pain as it hit her what he was saying. "Blackmail?" she said, whirling around to confront him. "Is that what you think I'm doing? Blackmailing you?"

"What do you call it?"

Annie was struck to her soul. She stared at him helplessly as the horrors of the last five years began to assail her, flashing through her unguarded mind so vividly that she didn't even attempt to stop them. She'd thought them buried, those excoriating memories, buried under her savage need to survive, but they'd only been hiding, festering. "Blackmail?" she said, barely able to get out the word. "I went to prison because of you!"

"Prison? What are you talking about?"

It tumbled out of her uncontrollably, like poison from a ruptured wound. She couldn't stop herself from telling him all the brutal things that had happened to her after their car wreck, flinging the details at him like knives. "The secret police found me unconscious with our marriage certificate in my bag. They took me in for questioning, and when I couldn't tell them anything, they tried to make me believe that you'd saved yourself and left me for dead. They said you were an agent. They charged me with conspiracy and subversion."

"I didn't know!" Shock tautened Chase's voice. "I was told you were dead. What happened to you?"

She turned away again and closed her eyes, the rupture ripping apart like an old, tough scar. The hot pain that filled her was excruciating at first, flaring up as if to scald her alive, and then finally, mercifully, it was numbing. "No, I didn't die," she said softly. "But I didn't live either."

She knuckled away the wetness from her eyes, and felt Shadow's fur brushing her leg. That same aching loneliness welled up inside her as she knelt to pet the dog. She wanted to hug his quivering body close and cry until she was emptied of anguish. But she didn't dare. The hurt went deep, deep enough to shatter with the slightest pressure. There would be nothing left of her but broken pieces.

"Annie, what happened?" Chase pressed.

She looked up at him for a long time. At last she responded, "The nuns found out I was alive, and in custody. They got me out, but not before the police had their pound of flesh. They have some very ingenious methods of interrogation."

"Oh . . . God."

"It could have been worse, I suppose. They took into account that I'd lost my parents to the guerrillas, and that I was little more than a child. So they spared me some of the nastier inducements. I wasn't raped, and I wasn't physically tortured . . . much."

"Much? What did they do?" His fist clenched as he asked the question. "Annie, tell me."

"Starvation and isolation. When that didn't work, they threatened to break every bone in my face. They said I'd be so ugly, no one would ever want to look at me again." She pointed to the bridge of her nose. "They started here."

He shook his head, horrified. "Annie, I didn't know. You've got to believe that."

She turned to the dog, gathering herself. "I do," she said with some effort. But as she stood and faced him, a painful question formed in her mind. "Would it have been any different if you had known?"

His dark eyes and lean, rugged countenance took her back to a sweeter time, an indelible moment of courage, a memory of hope. But his hesitation hurt her so much that she looked away before he could answer. She didn't want to be robbed of her last illusion. At sixteen she'd lost everything—her parents, her identity, and him. The one thing that had kept her alive through the nightmare was the dream that he would come back for her. She still wanted to believe he would have if he'd known. She wasn't ready to let that dream die. And she wouldn't let him kill it for her.

Chase's overwhelming impulse as she stood trembling before him was to take her into his arms. There was confusion in his mind, conflict locked in his heart, but he was strangely beyond the reach of those concerns. He could feel the astonishing depth of her pain, and he was beginning to understand that he was at the source of it.

"Annie," he said, wanting badly to touch her. "When I woke up in the hospital, they told me you'd been killed. I had very little choice but to believe them. I couldn't remember anything that happened on that mission. I still can't."

She stared at him, her eyes swimming with pain as the pupils constricted to pinpricks. Even his explanation seemed to bring her anguish. "I'm sorry," he told her.

"Don't be sorry. It can't be helped now."

"No, maybe it can." He held out his hand to her. "Maybe it can be helped. . . ."

But Annie couldn't take his hand. She felt a stab of despair even at the thought. It was everything she'd longed for, the shelter of his arms, the warmth of his body, the strength. But she couldn't let herself accept his comfort now. She was too raw with memories. Too abraded by a past he couldn't share. If she went to him now, she would break apart inside.

"What's wrong?" he asked, stepping toward her.

"No, Chase—" She backed up against the countertop, unwilling to let him touch her. In her confusion she heard Shadow move in front of her protectively. A low growl reverberated in the dog's throat.

Chase hesitated, bewildered by the scene before him. The woman was acting as if she was terrified of him, as if he were some kind of monster. And his own dog seemed determined to protect her from him. A strange kind of sadness welled up in him; tension made his jaw lock. This was ridiculous. All he wanted to do was help.

"Annie, for God's sake, come here."

Annie shook her head. She had once told herself that if he ever said those words to her, she would go to him. That he would own her, body and soul. It was the truth then. . . .

Chase held up his hands, confused, frustrated. "Annie—"

Shadow whimpered, responding to the plea in Chase's tone.

A soft cry was trapped in Annie's throat as the Border collie tried to nudge her toward Chase. When she didn't move, he left her side and went to his master. She felt totally abandoned as she watched the dog brush up against Chase's leg and then turn back to her, his soft brown eyes pleading.

They were beautiful together, Annie thought, struck by the sight of the towering cowboy and his sad-eyed dog. They made a poignant statement.

"Annie," Chase said softly, huskily. "Let me help."

She averted her eyes as he walked toward her. She had no way to protect herself as he stood in front of her and drew her rigid body into his arms. He was such a big man in comparison to her, so solid and secure, that being close to him brought her need for tenderness into sharp and painful focus. It would have been wonderful to let go and relax in his arms, to lean up against him. But Annie couldn't let herself do that.

"Easy does it, Red," he said, drawing her closer, caressing her hair. "Easy."

His fingers were warm and light against her hair, and every touch brought her a bittersweet mix of joy and sadness. As much as she desperately wanted to resist him, she could feel herself softening a little, giving in to the gentle pressure.

But that frightening question had to be asked again. "Would you have come back for me?" she said suddenly, looking up at him. "If you'd known?"

He met her gaze and held it, rubbing gently at a smudge of dirt on her cheek with his thumb. "Yes."

Annie was filled with the sweet pain of that one simple word. How long? she thought. How long had she waited to hear him say that? Tears welled up, scalding and bitter. She was rocked to her very core, aching with something that must have been joy, and at the same time, afraid to let herself believe it was true. What if he didn't mean it? What if he was only trying to keep from hurting her? The conflict mounted, but she had waited so long for this moment, she was helpless to stop the onslaught.

"Thank you for that," was all she could manage.

He drew her closer, and as their bodies touched, she felt a little shudder go through him. Her response was spontaneous. For all of his tough cowboy ways and reckless sensuality, it was that one hint of vulnerability that melted her. She softened against him, resting her cheek against his chest with a nervous sigh, and hesitantly entwining her arms around him.

Chase closed his eyes, enjoying the silky feel of her hair against his neck and the tentative, frightened way she was allowing herself to rest against him. Other than a lost fawn he'd rescued once, she had to be the most vulnerable, trembling bunch of sweetness he'd ever held in his arms. She triggered all his protective instincts, but at the moment he wasn't going to worry about what it might mean. She needed holding. And he was glad to be the one doing it.

She broke away from him after a long moment, as though she'd had all the closeness she could handle. "Am I a mess?" she asked, touching her dirt-smudged face. "I must be."

"Let me see."

She looked up at him, her expression still tinged with sadness as he began to work on one of the smudges.

"It seems like I'm always cleaning you up, doesn't it, Missy?" Her response was simply to smile, and for some reason, that brought him more pleasure than he could have imagined. "I guess somebody's got to do it," he said.

As he continued to make her presentable, he became aware of her slowed breathing. There was a faint resonance to it, almost sandy, and very sweet. Annie Wells was a sexy breather.

And then it happened again, just like before. He was kissing her. Without having planned it. Without even knowing he was going to do it, he tipped her chin up and bent his head to hers. Their lips brushed once, lightly, with a rush of sweetness that made his stomach clench. And then he backed away for an instant, as though realizing what he'd done. His mind seemed to be telling him that he had one last chance to save himself. But instead of saving him, that moment's hesitation was his downfall.

With her head tilted back and her lips so near his, Annie Wells had to be the most tantalizing creature he'd ever had the pleasure of coming across. Or was it the misfortune? Her breath held a startled quality, but her eyes were heavy-lidded and limpid with sensuality, and her mouth . . . God.

"What are you doing, Missy?" Chase said harshly. "What are you doing to me?"

"Nothing, Chase. Nothing."

But that just wasn't true. She was doing plenty. Her lips were parted and moist, asking to be kissed. Her breasts were pillowing against his chest, and her thighs were nudging his. Everything about her was breathless and soft. And everything about him was rushing and hard. Or soon would be.

I must be setting records with this woman, he thought, feeling the familiar flash of heat in his loins. He couldn't remember ever getting so aroused so fast—even in his adolescent years when all it took was the mention of a girl's name to get him going. But it wasn't a question of getting started since she'd come into his life. The gun hadn't even fired, and he was already out of the starting gate.

"Maybe we shouldn't," she said, her breath bathing him as she murmured the words.

"No maybe about it," Chase agreed. But he closed his hand in her hair and gently drew her head back even farther, exposing the white skin of her neck and a delicate heartbeat at its base. "We shouldn't," he murmured, settling his mouth on hers again, a full kiss this time, lips meeting with a subtle, vibrant pressure across their entire surface. A lingering kiss, until he lightened it. "Should not," he whispered, drawing away, yet staying close.

Without thinking, he slid his hand to the small of her back and felt her arch in response. She averted her eyes, but a tiny sound came out of her—a sound that made him lean down and kiss her again, harder this time, answering the thunderbolt of sensation that struck his groin. He was breathing hard when he broke away. "We shouldn't even get near each other."

She nodded, breathless, too, but seemingly sincere. "Which one of us is going to stop?" she asked with a dart of her tongue wetting the lips he'd just kissed. Perhaps it was an unconscious reflex on her part. He didn't know. He didn't care. He kissed her again.

Me, he thought, as he truly took possession of her wanton mouth, penetrating her parted lips in search of the tongue she'd given him a glimpse of, driving deeply with his own tongue, probing, tasting. I'm going to stop. One of these days. Right after I've had enough soul-satisfying sex with this woman to put me in my grave.

"I'll stop," he said, gathering her up in his arms, hugging her close in a surge of male energy. "Leave it to me." Heat thrummed violently into muscles that were already taut. Blood steamed through his veins as he broke the pounding kiss and cupped her face in his hands, stormy in his need, tender as he saw the apprehension in her eyes.

"I am going to stop, Annie," he said, making an effort to gentle his voice. "But not until I'm damn good and through with you. We'll call it quits when we've had as much pleasure as we can stand." Without a beat he bent and hooked an arm under her knees, lifting her.

Annie clung to his neck as he carried her to the cot. Her heart was knocking, and there was a deep throb of anticipation in the pit of her belly. But if she was shaking with desire, she was also confused by the faint stirring of alarm she felt. This was what she wanted, wasn't it? To make love with him? Of course it was, she told herself. This was the way she'd planned to help him remember, to strengthen the bond.

She was more aware than ever of the disparity in their height as he settled her on the cot and stood above her, unbuttoning his shirt. He was as tall as a small tree, and wonderfully lean, with the tightest, sexiest muscles bulging everywhere. Annie felt a hot blush of embarrassment at the explicitness of her thoughts—and realized she could think anything she wanted about Chase Beaudine—she was married to him.

But how did a large man make love to a tiny woman, she wondered, without crushing her? She knew about women dying in childbirth. She'd been a witness to such things in the jungle, but she'd never heard of a woman being killed by having sex.

That possibility began to seem more and more likely as Chase leaned over to pull off his boots and then straightened again, stripping off his shirt. His shoulders were broad and heavily muscled, and one of his hands could make two of hers. But it wasn't until he'd undone his jeans and was tugging them down that she became genuinely nervous. He wasn't wearing underwear, so she had no time to prepare herself for what she was about to see. And no time to stop the gasp when she saw it. Perhaps it was the state of his arousal, but Annie knew for sure that her days were numbered when she got a look at the proportions of his male organ. Even if she didn't die by being crushed into dust, she would certainly have to be put out of her misery when he got through with her—if he intended to use that thing!

Chase heard her gasp and knew he had some reassuring to do. He was used to women being nervous about having sexual dealings with a big man, but he'd learned how to ease their concerns. In fact, most of them had been pretty happy afterward.

"I guess we're not in any hurry, are we, Red?" he said, drawing his jeans back on as he sat down next to her. He touched a curl that had strayed onto her flushed cheek and then let his hand drift down toward her mouth. "Why don't we start with you?"

"With me?" Annie touched the neckline of her sweater as she realized what he was suggesting. "All right then," she said after a moment. "Let's start with me." Steadying her hands, she began to unbutton her sweater, purposely starting at the bottom instead of the top.

He halted her efforts with a touch. "I'd like to do it, if it's all the same to you."

She dropped her hands away, granting his request with a taut sigh and a deep flutter of abandon. It seemed like a small surrender, letting him undo her buttons, but the prospect sent a thrill of fear through her. Or was it excitement? She couldn't tell anymore. And she couldn't help but wonder what was going to happen to her in the arms of such a man. And in his bed. Would she survive the experience? She'd been through life-and-death ordeals since birth, but for some baffling reason, this felt like her test of fire—as though all of her experiences had been building to this one, to this man and this moment.

The buttons seemed to fall open under Chase's long fingers, and before she could catch a breath, he had laid open her sweater and was regarding her with eyes so black, it hurt to look at them. Reaching out, he fingered the strap of her shift. He seemed intently focused on the embroidered pink words that were stretched over her full breasts as he eased two fingers under the strap, drew them down, and then slipped them inside the thin material where it was cut out at the armhole.

His fingers caressed the side of her breast, riveting her. He stroked her tingling flesh almost absently with the back of his forefinger, studying the proverb and never once looking at her. Each stroke felt hot and sweet against her skin, and somehow very illicit.

She gasped inwardly as he drew his hand out and cupped her breast, taking its weight and fullness into his palm. He curved his large hand to her tender flesh, burning her through the pink-and-white barrier of the shift. A moment later he raised his dark eyes to hers.

"Are you virtuous, Annie?"

"Is that . . . what you want me to be?"

His fingers moved caressingly. "Right now I want

you to be closer to me. Move forward, Annie, so that I can touch your other breast."

Something shimmered and coiled and pulled tight low in Annie's stomach. It was a strange, beautiful, weakening impulse beyond her control. She did what he asked. She had no choice. Excitement was coursing through her with the power of a deep ocean current. As she swayed toward him, she closed her eyes and felt her breathing go soft and shallow. The touch of his hand sent shocks of pleasure tumbling through her. Her breasts throbbed and her nipples peaked as he urged her closer and kissed her mouth.

It was a lazy, languid kiss, but the yearnings building deep within Annie were anything but lazy. She was melting inside. She was dying to make love with him, no matter how big a man he was. She wanted him terribly.

He drew back, releasing her. His hands settled on the neckline of her sweater as though he was going to take it off, but she arched up against his lips, refusing to relinquish his mouth as he began to remove her clothing. She had never, ever, felt this way before. She was intoxicated by the sensations flowing inside her, she was drunk with ardor. She couldn't bear to have him leave her for a moment. She needed his hands, his mouth.

A low moan caught in her throat as he broke the kiss and began to draw up her shift. "I know you never take this off," he said. "But I want you naked when I make love to you."

Annie knew vaguely that the shift was her last defense, her only remaining protection against the feelings that were overpowering her. Removing it would strip her of all reason and resistance. She knew that, but the knowledge didn't help her when he asked her to raise her arms.

"I can't."

Her arms felt too heavy to lift, but she must have done what he wanted, because a moment later the shift was gone, and he was taking her breasts in his hands again. She felt the coil of desire tightening inside her. It clutched at her sharply, sweetly, and yet everywhere else, her body was weak and melting. She felt as if a tropical fever were washing over her, burning her skin with heat and spiraling her down into sweet and total oblivion.

His hands were at her waist, and then he was lifting her hips, pulling off her jeans. She moaned as he dragged her down on the bed, opening her legs. And then suddenly he was above her, his dark eyes boring into her dazed and dizzy thoughts, and there was an unfamiliar pressure between her thighs.

Chase had to fight back some demons as he gazed at the naked creature lying beneath him. She was a child-woman, innocently wanton, abandoned enough to ruin any man's intentions, no matter how good. He could easily have got rough and possessive with her. Hell, he *wanted* to get rough and possessive. He was potent, throbbing. All of his impulses were telling him to show no mercy, but he knew the pleasure would come in pleasuring her, and Annie Wells was tiny. He wanted her to have every exquisite sensation he could give her, and that meant slowing things down to a crawl.

Once he'd stroked open her thighs and positioned himself inside them, he rocked forward gently, sliding his hands under her hips and scooping her up as he pressed against the sweetest, tenderest part of her body. She threw her arms around his neck, her fingernails digging into his back as he entered her, easing into her with the tip of his shaft, probing and pushing, penetrating a little at a time.

Chase closed his eyes at the grabbing, clutching pleasure of it all. Now he knew what it was like to be a powerful engine with the brakes on—a locomotive throttling down. It was hell going slow with a hungry woman. Glorious hell.

At her writhing insistence he inched a little deeper, and felt a tightness that made him pause. At first he thought it was her muscles holding him back, but as he probed further, he knew it was something else, a physical barrier. The awareness came slowly at first, and then the shock of it caught him all at once. She hadn't made love with him before. She hadn't made love with anyone. Ever!

A wrench of sexual longing hit him, hardening to steel that part of him that was pulsing inside her. He wanted to say the hell with it, to finish what he'd started. His body wanted that satisfaction, too, no matter what the consequences. But even in his state of need and confusion, he knew there was too much at stake. It wasn't merely her virginity, although that alone would have been enough to stop him. It was what the act would mean now that he knew it was her first time.

"Annie," he said, cupping her face in his hands in an attempt to make her listen. "Why did you let me think— Annie, why didn't you tell me the truth?"

She stared up at him, bewildered. "What?"

"That you've never been with a man before."

She averted her eyes, but not quickly enough to hide the emotions that stormed through them—love and longing, guilt and despair. "What does that matter now, Chase? I'm here, and I want to be with you."

"Annie, for God's sake, you're a virgin."

She caught at his hands, a note of anguish in her voice. "Why does it matter that we didn't actually make love? We did get married. We said the vows."

Chase studied her flushed, urgent expression, the stab of longing in her eyes—and knew he had to call an immediate halt to the proceedings. If he stayed inside her for one more heartbeat, he was going to make love to her. Fully, totally, passionately, in every way, all the way, in as deep as he could get. And it wouldn't stop with her body, he knew that. He wouldn't be satisfied until he had all of her, every beat of her heart, every sigh in her soul.

He touched her face, regret surging through him as he withdrew from her. She flinched but made no attempt to stop him. Their knees bumped, and it was painfully awkward as he moved around her, but neither of them spoke. A moment later he was sitting on the cot, his back to her, wondering what in the hell to do.

She broke the silence. "Yes," she said, touching his shoulder, her fingertips cold. "I am a virgin, Chase. I've never made love before. But that isn't a bad thing, is it? I've never been touched by anyone since you touched me."

Never been touched by anyone since you . . .

Sweet Jesus, Chase thought, what the hell was happening? He rested his head in his hands, painfully aware of the throbbing condition of his body. And the heavy thud of his heart. One way or another, Annie Wells was going to be the undoing of him. He'd sensed that the moment he set eyes on her, and now it was all coming true. There was only one way to solve this problem. He had to get away from her. He had to get out of this house. And get out now.

Eight

"Living," Annie said, a sigh in her voice, "is like licking honey off a thorn." She wasn't sure where she'd heard that particular proverb, probably not the convent, but she'd never been more aware of its meaning. Even if the honey was as mouthwatering as you dreamed it would be, there was always the thorn. . . .

Chase was gone. He'd left two nights ago, right after their disastrous attempt at lovemaking. He'd packed up his clothes, his gear, and driven off in the Bronco, without telling her where he was going, or when he was coming back.

Annie's own sense of guilt had kept her from saying a word to stop him. She had misled him, there was no denying that, but she hadn't done it maliciously. All along, she'd held out the foolish hope that by the time they made love he might care about her enough that her virginity wouldn't matter. She'd even imagined that a man might be flattered by the fact that a woman had waited her whole life for him, and him alone. Not Chase. He'd done everything but run naked and screaming into the night.

Annie felt the nudge of a wet nose, and she draped an arm around the solemn dog who was sitting next to her. Shadow was her mainstay these days. Her one-sided conversations with the dog had become long, involved discourses on the pitfalls of trying to deal with a man who didn't want to be dealt with. It didn't occur to her to feel awkward about talking at such length to an animal. The *indígenas* of the rain forest had always believed in the existence of animal spirits, and Annie had no one else to talk to anyway.

She'd even confided her most guarded dream, the one she was afraid to let herself dwell on too much for fear that it might never come true. Only in the loneliest of the moments when she needed something to sustain her did she allow herself to fantasize about the moment when Chase would finally realize he cared.

"So, what's the answer?" she said, massaging the dog's neck as if bringing him comfort might bring her some. "Is this mission of mine a lost cause?"

Shadow graced her with one of his melancholy looks, and Annie felt as if she had a burr stuck in her throat as she hugged him. He seemed to be confirming what she already knew. That Chase wanted her out of his life, and there was nothing she could do to change his mind. Every attempt she'd made to get closer to him drove him further away.

Though it wasn't in Annie's nature to admit defeat, the harshness of her life in Costa Brava had taught her many lessons in survival. She knew there came a time when you had to let go of things beyond your control. Holding on to what was hopeless only compounded the pain for everyone concerned.

Had that time come for her? She rose to go inside, inexpressibly sad. Back in the cabin, she gathered up the few things she'd brought with her, trying to decide what she would do if she left.

As she glanced around at the kitchen she'd worked so hard to brighten up, she remembered vividly the way Chase had taken her into his arms, the way he'd kissed her. He wasn't immune to her physically. And if the emotion in his eyes wasn't longing, it was still breathtakingly intense. She'd seen passion, need, tenderness. He'd even shuddered when she'd rested her head on his chest. "Those weren't the reactions of a man who didn't care," she thought aloud.

The significance of those words didn't hit her until a moment later while she was walking down the hallway to the bathroom for her toiletries. She stopped short in front of the bathroom door, the realization still tugging at her, urging her toward an awareness that left her slightly thunderstruck when it finally hit. Maybe that was exactly the point. He *did* care. Only he didn't want to. He was fighting the feelings. And if the intensity of his reactions was any indication of the depth of his feelings . . . maybe he cared a great deal.

Her pulse broke into a gallop. No, she told herself instantly, afraid of the tumult building inside her. That kind of thinking was absurd—wish fulfillment, at best. She was inviting more pain.

She tried to still the chaotic pace of her thoughts, but propelled by her racing heart, they heaped example upon example in support of her crazy conclusion. The way he'd insisted they were rushing things, the way he'd stormed outside when she was undressing, his smoldering fury when he caught her coming out of the shower. It was all beginning to come clear, like shutters opening on a bright morning. More and more of Chase's erratic behavior made sense as she pondered it in the light shed by her insight. It even seemed possible that was why he'd run off. He couldn't deal with the force of his feelings.

As the next bombshell hit her, she threw out a hand, propping herself against the doorframe for support. Mother of Mercy, was it possible? Was there any chance, even the slightest, that he might be falling in love with her?

Chase Beaudine in love?

When cows climb trees, she thought. But she made a complete turn in the hallway and stared at the cabin's front window, entranced by the silvery moonlight streaming through the sparkling clean windowpane. What if everything Chase had done to prove he didn't care only proved that he did? What if all of that anger and denial, all of that surliness, was a manifestation of his internal struggle? If that was true, and if his obnoxious behavior was any indication of his real feelings, the man surely was in love. Passionately. Maybe even madly.

Annie walked to the front door and threw it open, staring out through the darkness at the road that had taken him away. She didn't want to delve too deeply into her realizations at that moment. They were too new, too fragile. And yet they'd come upon her so forcefully, she wanted to think they'd been inspired by divine guidance. It seemed the insights in themselves were a sign. She'd been seeking an answer, and she'd been given it.

If she was right—and with every breath she felt more confident that she was—then what she had to do now was find a way to explain all this to Chase. She had to help him understand what she herself was just beginning to understand.

"You got yourself a case of the Wyoming flu, partner?"

Chase gave the bartender a nod that succinctly communicated his state of mind. Yes, he did have himself a case of the Wyoming flu—which was also called a hangover in these parts; he needed some hundred-proof care, and he wanted to be left alone while he drank it.

"Looks like you could use some t'rantula juice," the bartender said, chuckling. "Shame I ain't got any."

Chase glared at the man, who quickly poured him a double Jack Daniel's and pushed it across the counter. The whiskey seared a path down Chase's throat like a blowtorch and ignited a fiery furnace in his gut. A moment later the alcohol's blue heat had numbed his throbbing forehead, and even thawed his icy heart a little.

An auburn-haired barmaid sidled up next to him, resting her chin on her palm and wrinkling her nose. If that was meant to be a smile, she needed some practice, Chase thought. But he did nothing to encourage her. He'd come to the Prairie Oyster to escape women and their interfering ways.

Chase downed the rest of his drink and pushed the empty shot glass back to the bartender for a refill. Women. They messed with men's cars and froo-frooed up their houses. They invaded a man's privacy, disordered his thinking, and stole away his dog's affections. A woman couldn't leave life the way she found it. She had to screw around with the natural balance of things.

"Women are creating a new endangered species," he said, directing his damning prediction toward the barmaid. "Men."

"I beg your pardon?"

Chase concentrated on his fresh drink, ignoring both the woman and the commotion that had just broken out near the entrance of the bar.

"Would you just look at that," the barmaid murmured, indicating the fracas Chase was trying to ignore. "Shame on them bullies, picking on that cute young fella. I'll bet he doesn't have himself such a jackass attitude about women."

Chase swung around to look, more to get the barmaid off his case then because he was interested. The commotion had moved to the center of the room, where a half-dozen cowpunchers down from one of the local ranches had encircled the newcomer. Chase eyed the young man in question, noting his outsized Stetson and denim jacket. He was a skinny kid with dirt smeared all over his beardless face and a jawful of chewing tobacco.

"You old enough to be in a bar, junior?" one of the cowpunchers asked, tapping the kid's Stetson.

The kid nodded, chewed hard on his tobacco, and spit out a wad of bug juice. The brown stuff landed with an impressive splat on the sawdust-strewn floor. A murmur of approval rippled through the room. And the kid kept chewing, vigorously.

"Damn poor velocity, kid," a second cowhand challenged. "Hock it up big, if you can, and let that there wad fly."

The kid nodded again and made a disgusting noise, screwing up his face and spitting hard. This time the juice went wide, but it still managed to clear the first shot by a foot. There was another murmur of approval, and someone at the bar even suggested getting the kid a beer. But the cowpunchers weren't satisfied.

"Not bad for a drip-nose runt," one of them sneered. "But the kid's got no aim a'tall."

The barmaid sashayed toward the circle of men, batting her drugstore eyelashes at the kid. "Bet you can shoot straight when you want to," she said, giving him the once-over. "That right, cowboy?"

The kid swallowed, and went slightly pale.

"You didn't answer the lady's question, boy," the cowpuncher said, flashing his cohorts an evil grin. "Damn if this Twinkie ain't impolite too."

"I'll bet I can throw him furthern he can spit," bragged another one. "Let's shag his skinny ass out of here."

The cowhands began to close in on the kid when someone at the bar yelled out, "Hold it, boys! First, ask the kid if he's a boy or a girl."

The saloon came alive with whistles and catcalls. Being called a girl was the ultimate insult to a macho cowboy. Now there was sure to be a fight, thought Chase, getting interested. He recognized the cowpuncher who was leading he fray as the man he'd caught "mending" fences. And the heavyset, mustached man at the bar was the foreman at the McAffrey ranch. He was drinking a glass of blue chalky stuff, and some of it had tipped his mustache white. But Chase was far more interested in the kid, who was also beginning to look strangely familiar to him.

Chase swung all the way around and rested the

back of his elbows on the bar, studying the scene. The kid worked his mouth ferociously, readying himself like a pitcher on the mound. Finally he dragged up a hock from hell and blew a blackish projectile that looked as though it were going out of the ballpark. Trouble was, there was an obstacle in its path. The foul wet wad caught the "fence mender" at close range, hitting his mail-order shirt with a sickening splash. Tobacco juice flew every which way, splattering several of the other men in the circle.

"Why, you little lizard turd," said the befouled man, grabbing the kid by the lapel of his jacket.

A second man reached into his boot for a weapon, but before he could get the knife free, there was an earsplitting crack of sound, and the blade went flying out of his hand. The disarmed man spun around, astonished. And at the same time, the entire bar turned to look at Chase Beaudine. He was drawing back the rawhide thong of his bullwhip, a look of hellish calm and deliberation in his eyes.

"Now that we've settled that matter," he said, addressing the cowpunchers, "I'd appreciate it if you boys were to back off. I'd like to deal with this 'Twinkie' in my own way."

"What's this got to do with you, Beaudine?" one of the cowhands said, a cigarette dangling from his fleshy lower lip.

The whip flashed out, an underhand throw that cut the man's cigarette cleanly in half not an inch from his mouth. "I've got a score to settle with the kid," Chase said. "Any problem with that?"

The room went silent as Chase yanked the whip back and wielded it one last time, wrapping it around the kid's waist. The kid looked greenish at the gills, and completely stunned. He dug in his heels, not going anywhere if he could help it, which nobody would have blamed him for in this case. But Beaudine had other ideas. He tugged the kid forward with a hard jerk.

Chase made no attempt to be gentle as he reeled in

the reluctant fish he'd hooked. As soon as the kid was close enough, Chase caught hold of his jacket and dragged him close, letting the whip uncoil and fall away. "I hope you've got a damn good reason for pulling this stunt, Missy," he said under his breath. "Because I'm not pleased."

Annie's mouth was so stuffed with chewing tobacco, her voice was little more than a gurgle. "I can s'plain," she managed.

"Damn right you can," Chase said, glancing around the room and gauging his chances of getting out of the place without a fight. "But not here." The saloon's back door was the nearest exit, and it opened onto an alley. "That way," he said, gathering up the whip as he pushed Annie toward the door.

Every bloodshot eye in the bar watched them make their exit. The foreman from the McAffrey ranch seemed particularly interested in Annie. "I swear I've seen that kid before," he said, "in Vern Sweetwater's drugstore. If that's a man, then I'm the queen of Sheba."

The barmaid threw in her two cents. "Well, just no wonder Chase Beaudine can't be bothered with redblooded, double-breasted females. He likes funkier stuff."

"Come on," Chase said to Annie, once they were in the alley. "The car's around front, parked on the street."

"Can I get rid of this chewing tobacco?" Annie called after him, tugged along in his wake as they jogged through the alley. "My stomach's getting queasy."

"Your stomach ought to be queasy after that fiasco," he said in a tone so low it was little more than a growl. "Spit out the wad and keep moving," he ordered. "I want you out of here before that bunch of yahoos decide to make you their mascot."

Annie took his advice to heart, promising herself that she would brush her teeth and rinse out her mouth about a hundred times starting the minute she got back to the cabin. For now she intended to follow Chase's orders to the letter. He was probably mad enough to murder her himself, but at the moment he seemed preoccupied with saving them both from embarrassment. And she wanted to keep it that way.

"But I rode into town on Fire," she told Chase, both of them breathing hard as they reached the Bronco. "I tied her up down by the feed store."

Chase unlocked the car door and waved Annie into the passenger seat. "That's okay, it's Tom O'Malley's store. He'll take care of her until I can get back into town to get her."

It wasn't until they were on the road and heading out of town that Chase unleashed the questions he'd obviously been holding in check. "Fill me in, Red," he said, his voice low and dangerously controlled. "I'm real curious about your reasons for crashing my private party."

Now didn't seem the moment to tell him that she understood all his crazy behavior, and that he was actually madly in love with her, so she offered a couple other reasons instead, which she realized were true the moment she uttered them. "I was worried about you, and . . . and I wanted to apologize for letting you think that we had made lo—"

"Don't remind me," he said abruptly. He glanced over at her, his eyes narrowing in pained disbelief as he took in her appearance. "What are you supposed to be, for God's sake?" His lips twitched as he asked the question, but his words sounded like snarls.

"I thought—I was hoping to be taken for a drifter. But I guess not, huh?" She removed the Stetson and shook her hair free. "Listen, I'm sure most of those people didn't pick up on that comment about my being a boy or a girl. And even if they did, it would only confuse them."

"Confuse them? You jump-started their batteries. They're probably taking odds right now on whether Chase Beaudine prefers cross-dressers or teenage boys."

Chase spiked the gas pedal and pulled out around

a horse trailer. The burst of speed reminded him how seriously ticked he was with her. Ticked enough to wreak some havoc, he thought, which meant he had better take a deep breath and bring it down. The possibility of being married to her was bad enough. He didn't want to do hard time for wringing her skinny neck.

As he roared down the road, he was tempted to continue the third degree. He was burning to ask her some questions, such as where she got the brass to do the things she did. And who the hell had taught her to chew tobacco. But what he really wanted to do was put the fear of God in Annie Wells. He wanted to see some bona fide contrition for all the grief she'd caused him, and he wanted it complete with tearful admissions of guilt and pleas for forgiveness. It would have given him the blackest, but greatest, pleasure to have her begging for mercy at that moment. And with that kind of fire burning inside him, he didn't trust himself to keep a level head if she gave him a wrong answer. Just one. That was all it would take.

Keep driving, cowboy, he told himself.

Annie absorbed Chase's taut silence uneasily. She was loath to initiate any conversation, but she was also profoundly curious to know what he was thinking—and if he had something dreadful in mind, like retribution. His stormy anger made her think of Sister Maria Innocentia's discourses on self-denial, mortification, and penance. Annie had never fully understood how mortification figured into the religious experience, but she was beginning to understand it where men and women were concerned. She and Chase seemed destined to mortify and humble each other.

"What are you planning to do?" she asked, making it a point not to look at him.

"About you? I don't know yet. And until I get it figured out, I'd suggest you don't give me any ideas. I'm half tempted to tie you up and lock you in the barn to keep you out of trouble. No, I'm *real* tempted."

Annie sucked in a breath and held it, not allowing herself to move as her heart started up with a painful jerk. "No, you won't," she said, her voice barely audible. She knew Chase was staring at her, but she didn't give a damn. She'd been through all the abuse she ever intended to go through in prison. She wouldn't let him, or anyone, tie her up, or lock her up, anywhere. Ever.

When she finally found the courage to speak, her voice was taut and trembling. "If I've done anything wrong, at least it was for the right reasons. I never meant to hurt you, only to help. And I never meant to make you angry. I was hoping to improve the condition of your life a little, to promote some happiness."

Chase had returned his focus to the road ahead, as though he didn't want to see, or be affected by, her emotions. "Well, do me a favor," he said, a hint of entreaty in his harsh voice. "Stop promoting my happiness. You're making me miserable."

The CB erupted in static, giving Annie a terrible start.

"Flying Nun?" a man's voice called. "You there, gal? This is Hopalong, your favorite road warrior."

Chase glanced at the microphone, confused.

"I think that's for me," Annie said. She reached for the microphone, but Chase beat her to it. His huge hand covered the mike as he stared at Annie. He looked for all the world like a man who'd just been diagnosed with a terminal illness—the disease being her.

Hopalong's voice shattered the ominous silence. "You still burning up the asphalt, baby?" he said.

Chase picked up the mike and stared at it, his jaw flexing as if he meant to eat the thing. Finally he hit the button and spoke into the unit. "The Flying Nun has had her wings clipped. Permanently."

Annie knew by the ferocity with which he hung up the mike and cranked the Bronco into a lower gear that her number had just been called. Chase Beaudine was going to skin her alive the minute he got her back to his cabin. Either that or he was going to kill them both with his reckless driving.

She closed her eyes and prayed for a miracle.

The ride to Chase's cabin was the longest trip of Annie's life. The atmosphere in the car was explosive. Chase didn't speak the entire time, and Annie kept herself busy mentally rehearsing how she was going to leap to safety if he headed for a cliff. When they actually pulled up in front of the cabin and he cut the engine, she gave silent thanks for answered prayers.

Chase jumped out of the car, leaving her there to contemplate the situation. She decided to give them both some distance and let things cool down. But a short time later, as she was letting herself out of the car, she was startled to see a dozen men on horseback come galloping out of the nearby hills. They were headed straight for the cabin, and the moonlight illuminated a silver badge on the chest of the lead rider. A pack of search-and-rescue dogs preceded the horses.

The thunder of horses' hooves brought Chase out of the cabin and down to the Bronco. "Looks like a manhunt," he said, signaling for Annie to stay inside the car and duck down. He retrieved his shotgun from the backseat and waited for the men as they rode up, their horses blowing and snorting.

"Saddle up, Beaudine," one of the men shouted. "We've got a jailbird on the run."

"Who is it?" asked Chase, addressing his question to the county sheriff, the man leading the group and wearing the badge. Most of the other men in the posse were either law enforcement or ranchers and members of the local Cattlemen's Association. Chase recognized several of the latter, including the foreman from the McAffrey ranch.

"Bad Luck Jack," the sheriff said, quieting his dancing horse with a pat. "Don't know how in hell he did it, but he made a break from one of my deputies' patrol cars. My man got waylaid on a burglary call while he was transporting Jack to the courthouse. When he got back to the car, the prisoner was gone."

"Seems like Jack's luck has changed." Chase's voice was suffused with irony as he thought about the times he himself had tracked down and apprehended Jack. The cattle rustler had a reputation for being as incorrigible as he was inept. "Got any idea where he's headed?"

The lawman tipped back his Stetson and scratched his forehead. "We lost his trail around Big Wash Canyon. Appears he might be heading for the state line, maybe thinking to cross the Canadian border by way of Montana. Thought you might like to get in on this, since you were the last one to bring him in."

Chase would have liked nothing better than to get in on it. Finally something he understood: riding horses and tracking down bad guys. The pungent smell of excited horseflesh and sweaty leather was permeating his senses. But manhunts often took days, and he couldn't leave Annie alone that long. No telling what his houseguest from hell would do with several days to kill! No one in the county would be safe.

"Sorry—not this time," he told the sheriff. "Got some things to take care of. But you hound dogs don't need me. You'll get your man."

"Have it your way," the lawman said, signaling to his men. "But you'll be missing all the fun. Let's go!" As all twelve started off, Chase followed their progress with his gaze. He would like to have been riding with them, but it was more than that. He couldn't help thinking that something was wrong with the strategy they had mapped out.

Inside the cab Annie waited for the sound of the horses' hooves to recede before she raised her head. "Are they gone?"

"Long gone," Chase said. "Come on out."

By the time she'd slid over to the door on his side, he'd opened it for her and was offering a hand to help her out. But she could see by the distant look in his eyes that his mind was somewhere else. "What is it?" she asked.

"I don't know. I've just got this feeling Jack's given those guys the slip. The last time I tracked him, I found him holed up in an old mine shack by the Cripple Creek Warm Springs. I've got a funny feeling he's gone back there again."

"Why would he do that?"

"Wish I knew." He shook his head. "Nah, it's only a hunch . . . unless he has something buried up there."

"Hunches are important," Annie said. "Maybe you ought to check it out."

"And leave you here? Alone? I don't think so, Missy."

Annie felt a small stirring of relief at the almost affectionate way he'd referred to her. Well, maybe affectionate was too optimistic a word, but at least he hadn't sounded angry. "If you're really concerned about leaving me here, that's easily solved. You could take me with you."

As Chase regarded her askance, she hastened to add, "But only if you think it's important to bring Bad Luck Jack back to justice. I know you're the one who put him in jail, and it must be frustrating that he's broken out, especially when you've got this hunch about where he is."

He considered her skeptically. "Take you along?"

"Just so you wouldn't have to worry about where I was and what I was doing. I wouldn't get involved, of course. I'd stay completely out of your way. I wouldn't even talk if you didn't want me to. Not a word."

He flipped up his Stetson and combed a hand through the exposed dark hair, thinking hard and looking as if his thought processes pained him greatly. Finally he swung around and headed for the corral.

"Chase? Where are you going?"

"To saddle up the horses. Get yourself a sleeping

bag out of the back of the Bronco and throw enough food and supplies together for both of us for a couple of days."

Annie closed her eyes and said a quick prayer of thanks. This is it, she thought. My miracle.

Nine

A majestic bower of blue oaks vaulted into the Wyoming night, blotting out the canopy of stars and filtering pale moonlight through their leafy arms. Where the trees thickened, the effect was a gloomy darkness, relieved only by hints of indigo.

After an hour on horseback Chase had allowed the nocturnal serenity to work its magic, tempering his mood a bit. He still wasn't sure he'd made the right decision to bring Annie along, but it beat worrying about what she might be doing on her own. Chase didn't want her alone in the cabin with an escaped convict on the loose. There was always the possibility that Bad Luck Jack might decide to pay a visit to the man who'd put him in jail.

The wind rose gently, creating a soft soughing in the trees. Lulled by the murmurous sounds, Chase found himself wondering how Annie was doing behind him. She'd been quiet the entire trip. He glanced over his shoulder. "Are you okay back there?"

"Yes," she said, as though surprised he'd asked. "I'm fine." A smile crept into her serious expression, and he realized how unused she was to consideration of any kind from him. It took damn little to please someone who had nothing, Chase thought.

And then realized he was thinking in platitudes, just as she did.

A moment later something made him glance back again, and as he did, he caught a mirrorlike flash of another woman, younger, almost a girl, her eyes wide with terror, her mouth twisted in a scream. The image was gone before he could discern any more details, but he knew who it was. Annie Wells, at sixteen.

He fought to bring her back, to remember—anything at all—but his mind jerked him to the present as mercilessly as it had dragged him into the past. With dizzying suddenness he found himself staring at a woman on horseback, at the Annie Wells he knew now. The moonlight was dancing in her hair; the night was casting shadows across her features, but he could see the confusion in her eyes as she urged her horse forward.

"Is something wrong?" she asked, riding up to him.

"No, I just thought I remembered something—"

"About me?"

The eagerness in her voice tugged at him, but he was feeling unsettled by what he'd seen, and he didn't want her probing further. "No, it was something else—someone else."

"Oh." There was a world of disappointment in that one hurt word. She let her horse drop back, and Chase had to forcibly remind himself to stay silent. The need to explain, to be of comfort in some way, was stronger than he cared to admit. As they continued their ride, a silence fell between them, accentuated by the occasional eerie cries of a pack of coyotes in the distance.

It was another half hour before they reached their destination. Chase tied the horses in a nearby grove of aspens and left Shadow to watch them while he set up camp on a bluff above the mine shack. The site he chose had an unobstructed view of the weathered structure and enough natural rock formations to protect him and Annie from the wind and weather.

The mine shack appeared deserted, but Chase's hunch about Jack grew even stronger as he settled himself against his rolled-up sleeping bag to take the first watch. Lying a few feet away on her own bag, Annie stared up at an inky sky, thick with twinkling stars.

She was so preternaturally quiet, Chase found himself glancing at her occasionally, and every time he did, his curiosity grew about the flashback he'd had of the terrified young girl. His former partners hadn't been able to tell him anything about the incident because they hadn't been there when he'd found her. Annie herself was the only one who knew the details.

He rested a hand on his thigh, feeling the ridges of the knife scar through the heavy denim of his jeans. "Tell me about Costa Brava," he said quietly.

Annie turned to look at him. "What do you want to know?"

"Where I found you. How I got this wound . . . everything."

Annie pushed herself to a sitting position on arms that were suddenly weak and shaky. She'd told him most of the story that first day in his cabin, but she'd been frightened and desperate to convince him who she was. He'd resisted everything she'd said then. Now it seemed he might be ready to listen.

"I'd be dead if it weren't for you," she admitted. She fought to keep her voice steady as she described how the convent had been under attack, bombed by *insurgentes*. She'd been hiding in the chapel when one of the rebels discovered her and raised his rifle to kill her. The man had her in his sights when suddenly the weapon was torn from his hands by Chase's bullwhip.

"He pulled a knife," she explained, describing the vicious battle that ended with the *insurgente* dead and Chase stabbed. Fortunately the wound was to his leg, and Annie knew enough medicine to apply a crude tourniquet and stem the bleeding.

Chase stopped her suddenly, his forehead ribbed

with concentration as he took up where she'd left off, recounting how they traveled hours to another village to find the priest, but by that time infection had already set in. "My leg was festering," he said, looking at her for corroboration. "There was inflammation, swelling, pus—"

"You do remember then?" Annie's breath rushed out as she waited for his answer.

"I don't know how much I'm remembering on my own and how much of it is mixed up with what you've already told me, but it feels like something I actually experienced. And the flashes I've had, they must be recall."

"Do you remember the fever setting in? The delirium?" If he remembered that, then surely he would remember the way she'd had to hold him to ease his convulsive shaking. Would he remember that she'd saved his life?

He shook his head slowly. "No . . . I don't know."

Disappointment swept her. *It's all right*, she told herself. He remembers some of it. In time he'll remember it all.

He looked up, still frowning intently. "You've told me about the rest of it—the marriage ceremony, the car wreck while we were heading for the border. I know it was the nuns who got you out of prison and gave you sanctuary. But you didn't tell me how you finally got out of the country."

"That was the nuns' doing too. They tried to find a way to help me prove my citizenship, but it got too dangerous. The country was constantly on the brink of civil war. The consulate was under siege, and foreigners, Americans in particular, were at risk. But the sisters were nothing if not resourceful. They hid me in the van of a truck that shipped cocoa, one of the country's major exports." She managed a smile. "It was a nightmare. Between secret police, guerrillas, and border guards, I was nearly caught several times. But, well, here I am."

"So you are," he agreed softly. "Must have been some kind of hell." He was silent a moment, and then his shoulders jerked with a self-deprecating sound, gallows laughter. "And I thought I had a rough childhood."

Annie was surprised at the bitter edge to his voice. "I guess we all do, don't we? One way or another. Growing up isn't easy." She recalled some of Chase's remarks about his father. He'd been delirious when he'd made them, and Annie had assumed he was having nightmares induced by the fever, but now she wasn't so sure. "Your father was an alcoholic, wasn't he?"

Chase fixed his eyes on the mine shack, as though weighing the wisdom of summoning up old ghosts. Annie remained quiet, determined to respect his privacy this time.

"Both of them drank," he said at last. "My mother too. I guess she figured if you can't beat 'em, join 'em. My old man was a mean drunk, and every time she complained, he'd knock her around. Pretty soon, she stopped complaining. After that I never saw her without a glass of booze in her hand."

"It must have been hard, having to watch that."

"Hard—yeah, that's one way of putting it. I did what I could to stop them, but all it got me was their undivided wrath. When they weren't beating on each other, they ganged up on me. Some days I didn't know if I was a kid or a punching bag. I finally took off at twelve, lived on the streets until I turned eighteen and joined the marines."

There was something harsh and terribly lonely etched into his profile. His jaw muscles moved with some painful memory, then tightened, locking it off. As he stared, unseeing, at the shack, Annie thought about the price he'd paid for his survival. She'd had some crushing experiences, but at least there'd been people around her who cared. He hadn't even had that. He'd had to face it all alone.

Now, as she studied him, one memory stuck out in her mind. He'd been delirious, ranting about his father. "Don't kill her, you bastard," he'd screamed, babbling an incoherent story about pulling his father off his mother during one of their fights. His mother had turned on her own ten-year-old son and attacked him for interfering. She'd beaten Chase with a broom handle, cracking three of his ribs.

At the time Annie hadn't been able to imagine family members inflicting that kind of pain on each other. Now she realized the story must have been true. Her throat constricted as she stared at Chase. *What kind of suffering had he been subjected to?* She drew in a shallow breath and held it, sensing the pain that would come when she exhaled. She wanted to say something, to bring him some comfort, but all she could think about was her own self-centered behavior. More than anything, she regretted the way she'd invaded his life and his privacy. She'd had precious little regard for anything but her own needs. She'd never once considered his feelings. Now she understood why he'd been so angry when she'd tried to turn his cabin into something resembling a home. The only association he had with homes, with family, was pain.

"Chase," she said, praying for the right words, "I know it's been miserable for you since I showed up. I can see that now, and I'm sorry. I wish I'd done things differently. I wish I'd never touched a thing in your place—and when we get back, I'll put everything exactly the way it was—"

"Let it go," he said almost gently, as though trying to head her off before the emotion got out of hand. "You had it in your mind to do a good thing, no matter how it turned out." He glanced over at her, letting his dark eyes settle on her for a moment. "There's no blame to be laid, Annie. None of this is anybody's fault. You came to me because you didn't have anywhere else to go."

Annie tried to speak and couldn't. She hadn't expected compassion, or anything close to it. "That's true," she said unsteadily. "I didn't have anywhere else to go . . . but I would have come to you anyway, Chase."

She hesitated, half expecting him to turn away.

When he didn't, she continued, needing to let out a little more of the aching truth that was stored in her heart. "It's just that I never forgot you, Chase. You came at a time when I'd lost everything. You risked your life for me, and I guess I fell in love with you back then. You know, the way a young girl does, her first crush, hero worship, that sort of thing . . ."

"Most young girls grow out of that," he said, returning his gaze to the shack.

His sudden lack of sensitivity caught her off guard. Was she imagining it, or had he closed the door before her very eyes? Even his handsome profile seemed to hold a warning now, a brooding reminder that he was a man who required distance. She felt the aching expand inside her, flaring hotly through her chest, and from what she knew of medicine, there was only one way to relieve the pressure—open the wound.

"Trouble is," she said, "I never did grow out of it."

He turned abruptly, his eyes wary. "Don't, Annie," he said, grainy-voiced. "Don't say something we'll both wish you hadn't."

But Annie couldn't stop herself. The aching swept into her throat like fire, impelling her. Even in the face of his husky warning, she whispered, "I love you, Chase. I can't help it."

The wind caught whatever it was he muttered as he rose to his feet and turned away from her. Annie didn't need to hear the words to know that she'd done it again, pushed things too far, pushed him away. She stared at his unyielding back and said his name softly, apologizing to him—and hating herself for doing it. Didn't she have any pride at all?

The pain felt as if it might split her chest open. She caught a hand to her rib cage, pressing hard as she struggled to her feet. If she could only get to some place where he couldn't see her, or hear her, she might be able to hold it together.

Her vision was blurred with tears as she walked toward the trees where the horses were tied. No one knew better than she that life had terrible lessons in store. Had she just come face-to-face with another one? There were people who couldn't love you back, no matter how much you loved them. They were incapable. Some dislocation, some fundamental betrayal of trust, had forced them forever off the path of normal relationships. She was deeply afraid that Chase was one of those people. He had been hurt too young, and too cruelly.

She had barely begun to breathe normally again when she heard the crackle of leaves behind her. Please, she thought, don't let it be him.

"Annie—"

She closed her eyes. "Let it go, Chase," she said, using his own words. "I don't want to talk, I can't—"

"Then let me talk, for God's sake. At least let me *apologize.*" His voice was thick with frustration. "Annie, I'm sorry. You caught me off guard, and I'm no good when it comes to surprises. I never did like surprises, okay?"

He touched a wayward lock of her hair, awkwardly, as though trying to smooth it. A savage word locked in his throat. "I don't know what the hell to say, Annie. I don't want to hurt you anymore. I don't want to take advantage—"

The tears she had conquered once welled up again. "Oh, Chase," she sighed, abandoning every shred of dignity as she turned to him. "Then don't say anything, dammit. Just go ahead and take advantage, why don't you? You won't be hurting me. I couldn't possibly hurt any more than I do now."

Chase stared at her in wary disbelief. Take advantage? What was she saying? He didn't know what to make of her, but that was nothing new. She didn't seem to be governed by the rules that applied to the rest of the human race. Even now, with her hair blowing onto her face and her fingers clinging to the neckline of her sweater, she looked as sweet and unconquerable as the day she arrived. His chest tightened, pressing in on him, threatening to cut off his oxygen. If he'd been able to resist her before, it was mostly through luck or circumstance. But his luck was running out.

"Do something, Chase," she said, her lower lip quivering irresistibly. "Anything."

He tipped her chin up with his fingers and searched her wild angel's face. "Okay, Missy . . . I'll do something."

Her eyes flashed a dazzling shade of blue, so vivid it resisted even the Wyoming darkness. "You *will*? You mean it?" She touched his arm, an entreaty in her voice. "Oh, please, Chase. Quick! Do it quick, before you change your mind."

"You are one loco woman," he said, pulling her into his arms. He brushed his mouth over hers, and she wrapped her arms around his neck, pressing herself to him, a frantic, squirming, insatiable thing. She appeared to be terrified that whatever he was offering her was going to be snatched away. He ran his hands down her back, all the way to her undulating hips, trying to gentle her some. Her mouth was so hot and sweet, he was loath to relinquish it ever, but she had other ideas. She broke the kiss.

"Do it, Chase, *please*," she said. "Throw me on the ground and do it—quick."

Laughter burned in his throat. He held her back a little, taking in her urgency, and increasingly aware of the tenderness building inside him. She brought out crazy impulses, powerful contradictions. Her squirming body was making him hotter than hell. He wanted to throw her to the ground and do it until they both went blind. But there was a deep, odd throb in his gut that kept him from giving in to the raw, animalistic urges.

"No, Missy, not quick . . . not that way. When we make love, it's going to be memorable. I'm going to be slow, and I'm going to be hard, and I'm going to drive you crazy."

Her mouth slipped open as she stared up at him. Neither of them spoke as he drew his thumb over the trembling in her lower lip. It was a slow, electrifying moment. The silence spun out around them as if time itself had paused, as if the cosmos were stopping to catch a breath. And then Chase bent to pick her up, and a profound gasp of relief came out of her as he swung her up into his arms.

"I think I'm already crazy," she said, clutching the back of his shirt. "But other than that, your plan sounds wonderful."

He settled her on her own sleeping bag, rolled out his bag next to hers, and zipped them together. By the time he was done, she'd already taken off her clothes and crawled into the bag. She smiled expectantly as he pulled off his boots, undid his shirt and jeans, and stretched out next to her, on the top of the bag.

"Annie," he said patiently, stroking her hair, "there are certain things a man likes to do once he's decided to make love to a woman, such as undress her, for example."

"Oh . . . I could put something back on."

He shook his head. "It's not the same."

"I could undress you."

"Then we'd both be crazy."

By the time he'd removed his shirt and jeans, Chase had decided to think of making love to Annie Wells as a challenge, not unlike some of the other challenges in his life, such as trying to get a saddle on an unbroken horse, for example. Annie was a whole lot sexier, but every bit as unpredictable. His only other thought before he crawled into the bag with her was that if Bad Luck Jack showed up, the rustler was going to have to entertain himself for a while.

Chase felt as if he'd touched a little bit of heaven as he curved his palm to the small of Annie's back and drew her toward him. Her skin was softer than the velvet of budding sage in the spring. It was warmer than clover basking in the sun. He brought his hand forward, letting it rest on the crest of her hip, resisting the urge to go further quickly.

The pleasure of holding back intensified as his mind took over, sending him flashes of a man's hand floating over sensual curves, barely skimming the surface before it touched down on quivering woman-flesh. His own body tightened hungrily as he imagined her response, her muscles tensing under his fingers, her startled moan as he stroked open her legs, feeding licks of slow, liquid fire to the inside of her thighs.

"Chase Beaudine? Are you daydreaming at a time like this?" She snuggled up against him as if she'd been made for that purpose, rubbing her silky breasts against his chest and locking her hips to his in a way that made him want to roll her onto her back and plunge into her, fast and furious. Deep and furious. Just plain furious.

"What else does a man like to do to a woman once he's decided to make love to her?" Annie asked. She was alternately twining her fingers in his chest hair and playing touchy-feely games with his parted lips as though she couldn't make up her mind which part of him to concentrate on.

"Any number of things—" Chase had already decided to give her a taste of the quick thrills she was asking for. With no more warning than a roguish smile, he cupped her breast, palming her roughly and flicking his thumb over the tender, erect bud. "This, for instance."

Annie felt a deep gush of desire. The heat and pressure of his palm, the scrape of calluses abrading her naked skin, were sweetly, urgently stimulating. A dark sensation shimmered and pulled tight in the pit of her stomach, coiling so vibrantly, it took her back to the day Chase demonstrated his prowess with the whip. She could almost hear the whipcrack, the quivering snap of black lightning, in her mind.

"But what a man really likes to do," he said, encircling her aureole with a languid motion, "is please the woman he's with. He likes to move along at her pace and let things work themselves out naturally."

Any other time Annie might have welcomed such an idea. But the way Chase was moving along, she was virtually certain that naturally also meant slowly, and the slower he went, the more her heart sped up, and the more her other parts leaped and shuddered with unbelievable urges.

"So we'll just take this thing in stages," he said. "How does that sound?"

"Fine, but could we skip a stage or two?" She drew up her leg, bumping his thigh. "I think I'm there already."

"Watch where you're putting that knee," he said, "or I might never get there."

Alarmed, Annie reached down to touch him, and her breathing got hung up for a second as she actually made contact. "Oh, my," she murmured. "You're there, Chase. You're there and then some. Does it hurt?"

He moaned something harsh and unintelligible. "It will, if you keep that up."

If Chase hadn't been in the condition she described, he was the moment her fingers began to stroke him. He tried to ignore the silky fire of her touch as he tipped up her chin to impress upon her why they had to take it slow. "Have you forgotten that we have a logistics problem, Annie? I'm built a little on the large side, and you're built small, remember? We tried this once before, and you weren't in such a hurry to 'do it' then."

Her skin color deepened, and though he knew he must have seen her blush before, he couldn't remember it being half as ravishing as now. Her fingers rediscovered his shaft as she spoke, bringing him a wrench of excitement.

"It's all right," she assured him. "I've had some time to get used to the idea since then, and I'm positive it won't be a problem, not even logistically. Nature knows how to handle these things. In childbirth the vagina can accommodate—"

"Annie! We are not talking about giving birth here. We're talking about making love. This is your first time, and I want you to think back on it as a pleasant experience."

Her fingers fluttered and went still as though she was determined to humor him. But she also looked crestfallen, and so urgently sexy, he decided to give her what she was fearlessly determined to have. "All right, on your back, woman," he said. "Let's put this male organ of mine to use."

"Really?" She rolled over and opened her legs, a smile tugging at her expectant expression. Her arms lay at her sides, and her breasts sloped gently away from each other, their weight spilling over her slender rib cage.

Good God, Chase thought. This woman slayed him. He'd had sex with quite a number of ladies in his life, but he'd never run into anyone remotely like Annie. She seemed completely free of the sexual tug-of-war that usually went along with lovemaking. She didn't play the games. She was just lying there, spread-eagled and blue-eyed, waiting, wanting him for all she was worth.

A jolt of desire rocketed through his body, slamming into his groin. If he wasn't careful, he was not only going to give her what she wanted, he was going to give it to her the way she wanted—fast!

He stretched himself out next to her, resisting the Bermuda Triangle of her open thighs. Once he got in there, he was a lost man, a shipwreck waiting to happen. "Annie," he said, lifting one of the coppery tendrils that had drifted onto her cheek. "I have this unreasonable need to kiss you. So indulge me, okay?"

She tilted her head up to meet the downward drift of his lips, her eyes closing. The way she sighed sent desire slamming through him all over again. Needing to take control, he cupped the back of her head and lifted her to him, burying his hand deep in her hair. Under the heat of his mouth, she tasted like every sweet, innocent dream, like every carnal urge he'd ever known.

With his free hand he captured the soft swing of her breast. She was full to overflowing in his hand, as lush and heavy with juice as ripened fruit. His stomach clutched as he pleasured her, working his long fingers, savoring the thrill as she arched against him and made an odd, plaintive sound in her throat, like the mewing of a lost and hungry kitten. Her mouth opened up under his, crying out to be filled.

He released her with a ragged sigh, staring into her eyes and letting his hand glide further south to the flattened plane of her woman's belly, to the mound of russet hair. He was testing, seeing how far she would let him go. Women always stopped a man at some point, if only to reassure themselves that they were in control. But as he stroked her crisp, curly hair and then cupped her mound, letting his fingers delve into the soft folds below it, he could feel her shudder under his touch.

"It gets even better, Annie," he said, searching for the tender bud at the core of her, the pleasure switch that would melt her nerves into warm syrup. When he found it, she began to undulate against him with plaintive little sighs. The mating sounds she made were barely audible, but they gave Chase his answer. She would let him go as far as he wanted. She was his to explore, to arouse, to possess . . . *in any way he wanted.*

The knowledge drove him crazy with lust. It racked him, pummeling him with heat and tenderness. He wanted to touch and kiss and suckle every wanton, undulating inch of her. In his mind he was already inside her, taking her virginity with deep, shuddering thrusts. His groin throbbed with the need for that satisfaction.

"Chase," she whispered, pressing herself against his hand, "I'm aching inside. Chase, do something!"

"It's all right," he said, easing a finger inside her as she strained against him. "I'll do something, I'll do more than that." He probed her taut muscles, working them gently, delving as deeply as her body would let him. A cry slipped out of her as he withdrew and reentered her with two fingers, checking her theory about accommodation. He found her warm and moist, throbbing with desire. If he needed any assurance that she was ready, he had it.

She murmured something that sounded like a prayer as he moved over her and positioned himself between her legs. Resting his weight on his hands, Chase pressed into the soft, delicate heat that was Annie Wells, and felt her natural resistance. "Easy," he said as she rocked against him with eager little thrusts. "Easy, Annie, that's what does it. Let your body decide when and how to take me. When it's ready, it will."

But Annie didn't share his patient attitude. She could feel him. Lord, she could feel him so vibrantly, the hardness, the solid width of him, as he pressed against her, nudging that tender, aching place, promising ecstasy. And whether her body wanted to take him or not, she did. She gripped his hips with her hands, aware of the flex of muscle, the dynamic tension in his flanks, as he probed and pushed, gentle but relentless.

She let out a little gasp as he entered her, hardened flesh pressing into soft, easing aside muscles that automatically tightened around him. Annie felt a wildness building, a whipcrack of excitement. She wanted to scream with pleasure and urge him on. But he stopped nearly as soon as he'd entered, leaving her that way, aching for more, only a little bit satisfied. It was torture, the cruelest form of torment she'd ever known.

"Chase, I'm dying. It's so sweet."

"We'll make it, baby," he said, his voice harsh. "Inch by inch, if that's what it takes."

Inch by inch, Annie thought. She'd never last that long! She kept her hands on his hips, thrilling to the flex of his buttocks as he moved inside her. Instinctively she began to explore him with her fingers, discovering that every inch of his backside was hardened and sleek to the touch. He was a man designed to bring a woman the most exquisite pleasure imaginable.

Now, if only he'd go a little faster! If only he'd truly make love to her instead of torturing her.

"Bring your legs up, Annie," he said. "Wrap them around me. Yes, that's it."

Annie was closer to getting her wish than she realized. As she entwined him with her legs, he gathered her up in his arms and pushed into her softness, all the way up to the barrier that had stopped him before.

"How we doing, Missy?" he said, his voice going harsh again. "You okay with that?"

"Yes, yes! I'm fine," she cried as he thrust again, a little harder this time. "It's not hurting at all. It feels wonderful, really. Oh! *Ouch*!"

"Easy now," Chase said, sliding his hands beneath her buttocks and scooping her up. "It'll only hurt for a minute. Like pulling off a bandage."

He thrust hard, and Annie's fingernails cut into his flesh as she felt a quick, tearing sensation inside her. It was more a sense of pressure than of pain, of something vital giving way, making way for a huge, intruding presence. There was one last thrust, and then the impediment was gone, and he surged deeply into her body. "Ohh," she gasped, feeling as though she were being opened like a channel, a river suddenly flowing free.

It was an enthralling sensation. She was aware of the entire length of him as he came to a gradual halt inside her. Lord, it felt as though he would stretch her to bursting.

"That's the worst of it, Missy," he said gently, holding her still while he bent his head and stroked her mouth with his. His breath was hot, his whisperings tender against her parted lips. A moment later, he was easing his way into her again, going just a little further with each flex of his hips. By the time he'd stopped completely, he was buried so deeply and exquisitely that she thought he must be touching her belly from the inside.

"I think we're there, baby," he said softly. "Are you all right?"

"I'm better than all right," she assured him. It had only hurt for a few seconds, as he'd promised. But that astonishing sense of pressure remained. And now she felt so wonderfully full, engorged. Dear God, it was rapture. "You are remarkably large, aren't you? I mean I knew you were, but I didn't realize . . ."

"And you've got a remarkably fresh mouth." Chase wondered if a cowboy was capable of blushing. He'd never had any false modesty about his size, but he'd never taken any particular pride in it either. However, now that she mentioned it, he did feel damn big inside her. Especially with her so tight all around him, and squeezing him the way she was. "You know what you're doing, don't you?" he asked. "You're hugging me, Missy."

"Sorry—"

"Don't be, it feels sensational." Chase closed his eyes, but as he tried to concentrate on the deep, pulsing pleasure, he gradually became aware of what else she was doing. Her wanton little fingers were roaming all over his backside. She was stroking and feeling and squeezing. As her fingers bit into his flanks, he tightened deep inside, his muscles jerking with pleasure.

"Annie, are you trying to tell me something?" he asked, tipping up her head and searching her face.

"Well, now that you ask," she admitted, wetting her lips as though to hold off a smile, "I was wondering about something. Are you going to move any time soon?"

"Would you like me to?"

"Oh, yes . . . ohh . . . *yes.*"

He rocked into her, moving slowly back and forth, and thrilling to the way she was able to take all of him, everything he had. Pleasure clutched deep inside him, giving way to a jolt of desire as she ran her hands down his back and cupped his buttocks. Her fingers dug into him, urging him deeper, faster. He'd been up against some rugged tests in his life, but holding off with this woman was the toughest, hands down.

He kissed her deeply, roughly, thrusting into her

mouth and into her body at the same time. Her hips rocked beneath him, and the soft bounce of her breasts was tantalizingly sexy. "Can you handle that, baby?" he asked. "I don't want to hurt you."

"Hurt me? I've never known such bliss."

Bliss, Chase thought, if that's what he was feeling now, he wanted to prolong it as long as was humanly possible. He wanted to overdose on bliss, to die of it, with her. He held out as long as he could, loving her with thrust after thrust, slow and sensual, deep and shuddering . . . until finally the hot throb of her hands and the urgent rhythm of her hips broke his control. She wanted it hard. She wanted it fast.

Give the lady what she wants, cowboy.

Annie couldn't hold back a sob of pure joy as he drove unrestrainedly into her body, gathering her up in her powerful arms and storming her with his animal passions. Nothing in her storehouse of fantasies had prepared her for the actual raw pleasure of making love with Chase Beaudine. The glorious pressure that had been there since he entered her was now deepening, tugging at her insides like a spring coiling in on itself, and at the same time, radiating sharp waves of pleasure. The urgent sensations fanned through her in tight little ripples.

As the coil shivered and pulled tight, her mind flashed a riveting image of black lightning. It jagged through the air, as hard and unforgiving as the crack of a rawhide whip. She could feel its heat and stinging sweetness in her mind. And then all at once, with the force of a thunderbolt, a whip cracked inside her and the coil of pleasure jerked unbearably tight. She writhed up, clutching at Chase with her arms and legs, until just as suddenly the coil broke free, reverberating wildly and leaving her gasping as it flooded her with spasms of incomprehensible joy.

She heard herself crying out Chase's name. She felt him shudder and drive deep inside her, and in her dazed, bewildered rapture, she wondered if he could possibly have experienced the same wonder as she had.

Ten

Chase sat on the outside of the sleeping bag, bare-chested, with one long leg drawn up as a resting place for his forearm. He wore only his jeans against the chill night air. Annie slept facing away from him, on her side, her body forming a soft S-curve inside the goosedown bag.

It had been hours since they'd made love, and from the look of the hills, Chase knew dawn would soon be breaking. He hadn't slept all night. His restlessness had nothing to do with Bad Luck Jack. The rustler had never shown up, proving Chase's hunch wrong, but that wasn't what had him concerned. He had a much larger dilemma at hand—namely, a red-headed, proverb-quoting, tobacco-chewing ex-virgin named Annie Wells.

He'd known making love with her would change everything, and it had. In the hours that had passed, he'd been mulling the consequences of that one seemingly simple act of passion. Taking her had been irresistible and imperative. Everything had demanded it, including her. But what did it mean? Even if he could convince himself that the act had been nothing more than a mutually satisfying, pleasure-driven moment, separate and distinct from everything else, he couldn't imagine her seeing it that way. She was probably dreaming about wedding gowns and honeymoons at this moment. With his luck and her timing, her fertile little body was probably already making a baby!

On that sobering thought his mind flashed from one bone-chilling consequence to another, including the requirements of the immigration service should he decide to acknowledge his hasty marriage to Annie. It wasn't as simple as filing a petition with the INS to grant her citizenship as his wife. The petitioning couple had to prove that their relationship was bona fide. Among other things, the agency required a two-year period of cohabitation.

Cohabitation with Annie Wells? Another bone-chilling thought. Just looking at her was enough to melt a man's heart, especially when she was asleep. She was sexier than original sin. But she was also haywire, noticeably so. Worse, she had an annoying way of imposing herself on every aspect of his life. A private man couldn't live like that. Chase had spent the last five years trying to simplify his life. In five minutes she'd reversed everything he'd done.

But the deepest concern he had on this chilly predawn morning—what bothered him more than any of the rest of his doubts—were her motives. She'd been so damn urgent about everything, including wanting to make love with him. If it had been a ploy to get him to commit, or to make him feel obligated, it had been half-successful. He damn sure felt obligated.

He pushed himself up and walked barefoot to the edge of the bluff, staring down at the deserted mine shack as he rubbed his hands together, working some heat back into them. Commitment. Now there was a word loaded down like a stock train headed for the slaughterhouse. Marriage, children, family, all linked up like boxcars. He could feel the weight, the straining bonds, of that much emotional baggage.

He didn't want bonds, of any kind. His parents had been bonded, perhaps by love at one point, but later by hate and mutual degradation. He'd seen how the ties got twisted, how they could strangle whatever was good in a person. If he'd devoted himself to anything in life, it was to avoiding emotional entanglements. Somebody always got hurt.

His problem was how to convince Annie of that. From what he knew of her, she would probably refuse to believe that she had run up against someone who didn't share her convictions. She believed in snails and arks and the unconquerable soul. Anything was possible with enough perseverance. Undoubtedly her proverbs had got her through some rough times, and he didn't want to be the one to destroy her illusions. But to him, they were nothing but crutches. Props to help a man convince himself that life had a rainbow waiting when the storm finally cleared.

He shuddered, hoping it was the cold and knowing it wasn't. He hated platitudes. It was cruel the way they kept a person holding out hope. They promised rainbows . . . and never delivered.

"Chase? What are you doing?"

Chase didn't turn around immediately. He didn't want her to see what he knew was written in his face—that what she wanted from him was impossible. Whatever there was between them, or might have been, was impossible. . . .

A muscle in his jaw tightened, aching hotly as he stared out at the hills, trying to figure out how he was going to tell her, but before he could find the words, she was next to him, pulling on her jeans and rushing to button up her sweater.

"What is it, Chase? The rustler?"

He shook his head without looking at her.

"Then what's wrong?"

"A lot, Annie. There's a whole lot wrong." He turned and gave her a taste of the kind of hurt he could inflict. Acid seemed to be pumping through the valves of his heart as he watched her concerned expression transform into something softer, sadder. The light was going out of her eyes. Hope was being extinguished by another emotion that had no discernible color. The irises of her eyes had shone robin's egg blue in the pale light, but now they were taking on an ashen dullness. Despair, he thought, that was the color of Annie's eyes. It made her heartbreakingly beautiful.

"You're sorry you made love to me, aren't you?"

"Annie . . ." Words rushed out of him, words that couldn't possibly bring back the vibrance to her eyes, but he said them anyway. "I'll do everything I can to help you regain your citizenship, if that's what you want. I've got some connections. I'll even swear out an affidavit that you're an American, or whatever it takes."

"Affidavit?"

"Yes, I'll get my partners to swear too—"

"But we're married, Chase. Why do we need affidavits?"

He turned away from her, trying to block out the naked hurt in her eyes. It ripped through his chest, it clawed at him, tearing out hunks of flesh. "Dammit, Annie, it's not going to work."

"What isn't going to work? Us?" Her voice softened, dropping off to a raspy whisper. "Anything can work if you're willing to fight for it. If you want it badly enough."

"For God's sake, would you try to understand?" He swung around to confront her, aware of his own impotent rage, his own searing sadness. There was only one way to deal with this hopeless mess. It was another bandage that had to be ripped off as quickly and painlessly as possible. "I don't want to be married, Annie. Not to you, not to anyone. I don't want a wife and yellow kitchen curtains and a pack of screaming brats underfoot."

The tears he'd expected to see sparkling in her eyes weren't there. Instead, she was looking at him with stunned disbelief, as if he were some kind of monster.

"It makes no difference to you that I'm in love with you?" she said. "That I always have been? None of that matters?"

"It all matters, Annie. It matters like hell. That's

why we've got to resolve this thing now. I can't let you go on thinking there's a future for us. We can't let this drag on any longer."

"We wouldn't have to stay married," she said, her voice growing distant, as if she was talking to herself more than to him. "We could be divorced as soon as my citizenship is a proven thing."

He turned away, raking a hand through his hair as he walked to the edge of the bluff. "Annie, the marriage in Costa Brava was a means to an end. It was a desperate measure, and we both know that. It may not even be valid, and if it is . . . it has to be dissolved."

Annie stepped back, staggering as a jagged rock cut into the sole of her bare foot. The pain was nothing compared to the brutal truth he was asking her to face. He didn't love her. He'd risked his life to rescue her, he'd even married her, but he hadn't loved her, then or now. *And he never would.* The fiery ache she'd felt earlier returned full force. It slashed a path up her throat and stung the lining of her mouth. The heat of it felt as much like anger as pain. And then she realized she *was* angry.

Arguments raged through her mind. She could think of a million ways to tell him what a selfish bastard he was, and how he was cutting himself off from everything good in life—from love, life's greatest happiness. But what would it accomplish? She would never be able to convince him he was wrong. His flinty gaze told her nothing she could say or do would make any difference. The door was closed.

Perhaps she'd been right about him—he wasn't capable of returning love. At the moment she didn't care. She just wanted to get away from him. Being in his presence was too painful. She hated the thought that she might have to accept his help with the immigration service, but she would deal with that later. For now, at least, she had to find a way to put some distance between them. "Chase, I'm—"

His hand whipped up, silencing her. The words backed up in her throat until she realized his harsh gesture was not meant to castigate her. He was staring down at the mine shack.

"There's someone down there," he said under his breath. He ducked behind the ledge, grabbing Annie by the hand and dragging her with him.

The sound of rotted boards being ripped loose with a crowbar drifted up to them. Chase ventured out from behind the cover of the ledge for a look. "I can't see who it is," he said, "but he's inside the shack. It's got to be Jack."

"Chase, I—"

Chase muffled her voice with his hand, pulling her close. "Not now," he whispered roughly. "It's not safe. He's probably armed."

Annie closed her eyes, hardly able to believe that she was enveloped in the warmth of Chase's strong arms, that her face was nestled in his soft, thick chest hair. His sheltering embrace gave her such terrible pleasure, such cruel pain. She broke away from him, refusing to let herself feel such things.

"Annie, please don't do anything stupid. Stay here while I check this out. Neither one of us is safe until I find out who's down there."

Annie watched silently as Chase pulled on his boots and shirt. Once he was dressed, he crept over to where the horses were staked out and lifted his bullwhip off the saddle horn. He also took a handgun from one of the saddlebags and tucked it into his leather belt. Then, motioning again for her to stay put, he started around the ridge toward a heavily treed section of the hill behind the shack.

As soon as he'd disappeared from Annie's sight, she felt a tug of fear and indecision. What if something happened to him? He could be hurt, or killed. A sense of dread overwhelmed her as she realized how helpless she was to do anything. What would she do if he died? No matter what had happened between them, he was still everything, her whole life.

And then, in the wake of her rising horror, the anger came tumbling back. And the tears. Caustic, burning tears. Damn Chase Beaudine anyway, she thought, knuckling the wetness away from her eyes. Damn him straight to the hinges of hell. He'd tossed her out of his life like damaged goods, and now he expected her to stand here and passively wait for him, wondering if he was going to live or die? No, she wouldn't do that. She couldn't. No woman could be expected to worry herself sick over a man who had just torn her heart from her body. That was too much. That was torture.

She found her tennis shoes underneath the sleeping bag and slipped them on as she tried to think what to do. More than anything she needed distance. She just wanted to get away from this place where heartache burned in the very air she breathed.

The horses nickered softly as she approached them, and Shadow roused from where he was sleeping. Annie knelt next to the dog, explaining to him that he couldn't come with her as she studied the saddles that Chase had thrown over a fallen birch tree the previous night. They looked as if they weighed almost as much as she did, and though Annie had never ridden bareback, it appeared that she had no other choice.

Untying the mare, she led her to the birch tree and used it as a step to climb aboard. Moments later, after several awkward tries, she was on the horse's wide, warm back, clinging to her halter and praying the animal knew the way back to the cabin.

The sun was breaking over the hills as Annie's mount veered from the path and set off across a meadow that looked vaguely familiar to her. She gave the horse its head, hoping the detour they were taking meant they were nearing the cabin.

Her legs ached from gripping the animal's ample girth, and her hands and arms were stiff from hanging on for dear life. There were other parts of her aching, too, but they had nothing to do with horseback riding. Her throat muscles felt bruised and sore from locking off wave after wave of sadness. And in another, deeper part of her body, she felt pried open and vulnerable in an entirely new way.

The twinges of tenderness reminded her of what she and Chase had done last night. And of how much she had loved the deep thrill of having him inside her. She had loved it so much, she was sure another man could never satisfy her now, and not simply because of physical proportions. Chase had been determined to give her more pleasure than pain, even if it meant sacrificing his own needs. He'd held back when she'd begged him not to because he'd known it wasn't time. Only when she was ready for the fullness of the act had he given in to her pleas.

He had ruined her for any other man, she thought, closing her eyes at the sharp spasm of pleasure. She would ache for him the rest of her life.

A low whirring of sound pulled her out of her troubled reflections. The mare's ears pricked, and suddenly she was moving faster, as though she'd heard the noise, too, and recognized it. As they crashed through a thicket of thimbleberries, Chase's small cabin appeared in the clearing ahead. The windmill that powered the water pump and generator was cranking around in the breeze.

Annie had to fight back tears of relief. She hadn't felt so grateful in a long time as she was to see that small, forlorn cabin nestled up against the hills. It looked and felt like home, though she knew she couldn't let herself think in those terms any longer.

After leaving the mare in her stall with fresh water and a bucket of oats, Annie headed for the house. The first thing she wanted was a long shower, as piping hot as she could get the water. Then maybe she could figure out what to do with the rest of her life.

Her spirits lifted a little as she bounded up the front steps, but the minute she opened the door and walked in, she knew something was wrong. There was a stillness in the room, a pulsing presence that told her she wasn't alone.

"Is someone here?" she said, halting midstride as a shadow loomed behind her. "Who is it?"

"I was about to ask you the same question."

The man's voice had a harsh resonance that brought gooseflesh to Annie's forearms. She whirled, and caught a quick impression of the intruder in the shadows thrown by the open door. She couldn't see him clearly, but he looked to be at least as tall as Chase. Darkness, that was the word that struck her as she tried to discern his features. The image of a black jungle cat flashed into her mind as she caught the glint of his obsidian eyes, and the long, dark hair flowing down his back.

"Where's Chase Beaudine?" he asked. "And what are you doing in his place?"

It hit Annie all at once who he was. Who he had to be! The rustler everyone was stalking. Bad Luck Jack.

"Chase isn't here," she said, stalling for time. She was already envisioning herself being taken as a hostage if she didn't come up with some way out of the situation. There wasn't any point in trying to get past him and out the door, but there might be a way to outsmart him.

"Where is he?" the man asked.

She let her eyes dart nervously toward the bedroom door. "I don't know," she said, sharpening her voice. "He's gone, that's all. I don't expect him back for some time. Days maybe."

She glanced again at the bedroom.

"Somebody in there?" He nodded toward the doorway.

"No," Annie said emphatically.

The man looked from the door to her and back again, then motioned her toward the room. "Let's check it out. You first."

Annie's pulse was throbbing in her forehead as she halted in the bedroom doorway. "There's no one in there," she insisted. "He's gone."

The intruder pushed her over the threshold none too gently and entered the room behind her. "What's that?" he asked, spotting the vault door immediately.

"Nothing, a back entrance—"

"Open it."

Moments later they were in the tunnel, Annie leading the way after lighting one of the rusty kerosene lanterns that had hung on the kitchen wall. The man behind her said nothing as they cut through the musky darkness; he just kept prodding her forward.

Once they'd entered the small open cavern, Annie hesitated to let him check out the area. As his eyes roamed the walls, she began to inch away from him, trying to hold the lantern steady so he wouldn't notice. "Look out!" she cried, hoping it would throw him off-balance as she ducked into the nearest tunnel and snuffed out the lantern.

She heard him stumble forward, and then came the sound she'd been waiting for: a harsh shout of surprise and the teeth-rattling thud of a large body colliding against hard clay. He'd fallen into the pit. Annie fumbled to find her matches and relight the lantern in the pitch-blackness. Once she had the wick glowing again, she approached the pit with great caution.

Her victim was sitting on the clay floor, rubbing the knee of his jeans, which was ripped out. She thought he seemed rather subdued until he glanced up. The luminous glare of his eyes froze her like a blinded animal. Lord, he did look like a jungle cat. "Who are you?" she asked. "Bad Luck Jack?"

His eyes narrowed as he stared up at her, and then a faint smile transformed his features into something a little less terrifying. "I have had better luck," he said. "But no, that's not my name. I'm Johnny Starhawk, an old friend of Chase's."

"You're *who*?" Shock crashed through Annie. He couldn't be Johnny Starhawk. She'd met the man in Costa Brava. He'd worn fatigues, aviator sunglasses, and the short-cropped hair of a marine. This man's hair was a flying mane that fell below his shoulder blades, and now that she could see him clearly, she realized he had a strip of rawhide tied around his forehead. He looked like a renegade Indian. But hadn't Chase said Johnny was a prominent lawyer?

She held out the lantern, peering down at the sensual arc of his cheekbones, the hard, flaring jaw and tawny skin. An irreverent thought entered her mind. Johnny Starhawk was gorgeous, she realized, smothering a quick smile. Too bad she was already in love.

"Chase left me an urgent message." He continued to rub his knee as he stared up at her. "Why do I have the feeling it has something to do with you?"

"Maybe I should explain," Annie suggested. She started with profuse apologies, hastening to add that she'd taken him for a rustler who'd escaped custody, and then informing him that she'd already met him once, five years before. "Do I look at all familiar?" she asked, holding the lantern up to her face.

"I could take a better look if you got me out of here."

"Oh, I'm sorry." She glanced around the cavern, realizing she had no idea how to get him out. "Chase has a rope ladder, but I don't know where he keeps it."

"Forget that for now," Johnny said, staring up at her as though he might be remembering. "You said we met?"

"Yes, in Costa Brava. I could tell you how it happened—"

"Please do."

Annie decided she rather liked the dry forbearance in his tone. The Indians she'd known in Costa Brava, though primitive by American standards, had been a very gentle people. This man looked anything but gentle, yet there seemed to be a streak of charm hidden under the pantherish darkness. Still, she was rather glad she had no way to get him out of the pit. It felt a little safer with the big cat in his cage.

There was a sensual indolence in the way he rested his head against the wall of the pit, watching her as though he was waiting for the games to begin. Annie

found herself talking quickly, urgently, as she recounted the details of their rendezvous on the way to
the border. She described the jeep Chase was driving, the clothing they wore, Chase's knife wound and
bouts of delirium. By the time she'd finished, Johnny
had risen to his feet, and his expression had transformed from dispassion to rapt disbelief. "You don't
remember me, do you?" she said, sharply disappointed.

"I feel like I'm staring at a ghost." He searched out
the details of her face through the murkiness. "So
you're the kid Chase married? Annie . . . Was that
your name?"

"Yes." The word shook on her lips. Emotion roiled
up inside her so suddenly, she couldn't control it.
Tears sprang to her eyes, and her taut facial muscles
crumbled with relief. She knew he must think she
was crazy, a woman gone completely out of her mind,
but he was the first person to recognize her. He'd
actually said her name, and that simple acknowledg-
ment felt like an affirmation of her existence.

"Yes," she said, "I'm Annie—Annie Wells." Mingled
with the joy, the pain, the shaking relief, Annie had
the oddest sense of being given the right to reclaim
her identity and her life, of being reborn in some way.
"Forgive me," she said, profoundly embarrassed. "I
was just so afraid you wouldn't remember me, that
no one would ever remember me again."

"Nothing to forgive." He waited a moment, studying his hands, respectful of her need to recover
privately. "We found Chase unconscious in the jeep
after it went over the embankment," he said quietly,
"but you'd been thrown free. All we ever found was
one of your shoes, floating on the river."

"I know. Chase thought I was dead all these
years."

"I'll bet you gave him one hell of a surprise."

"Yes. I did." Annie's smile went crooked. She could
feel tears threatening again, and she fought them
back, determined not to embarrass herself any further. But she couldn't stop the sigh that welled up

when she spoke. "Chase doesn't remember me. Or anything that happened between us down there. He wants the marriage . . . dissolved."

Johnny studied her. "And you don't, right?"

"I love him," she said, the words tight, aching. "I guess it shows, huh?"

"You can't even say his name without sounding like you're praying. Yes, it shows, Annie. What's going on?"

Annie needed very little encouragement to pour out the whole sad story. Somehow she held her hurt and anger in check as she gave Johnny Starhawk a blow-by-blow account of the chaos that had erupted since she'd arrived. But the more she talked, the more she realized anew how thoroughly she'd disrupted Chase's life. "I guess it's no wonder he wants me gone," she said. "I've brought him nothing but misery. He said so himself."

"Don't be so sure," Johnny said, grinning.

"What do you mean?"

As Johnny Starhawk registered the strange, changeless beauty of the child-woman hovering above him, the sweet suffering in her blue eyes, he couldn't imagine how any man could resist her, even a hard case like Chase Beaudine. "No promises, Annie," he said, "but I've got a couple of ideas on how to handle my ex-partner."

Eleven

"*Freeze*, Beaudine! You even blink, and I'll shoot you where you look the biggest."

The harsh command came from just over Chase's right shoulder. Chase hesitated in midstride, his boot crunching down on a chunk of broken glass. "You always were a lousy shot, Jack. Even with a life-size target."

"At this range I could blow your head off blind-folded."

Dead to rights, Chase thought, his lip curling with disgust as he surveyed the rotting innards of the mining shack. The bastard had caught him dead to rights. Jack must have seen him coming around the back of the cabin, snuck out the front, and come up behind him. Chase considered some kind of coun-termove, like going for the rustler's gun. But Jack did have a point. Even he couldn't be expected to miss at such close range.

"Drop the bullwhip, Beaudine." Two sharp clicks sounded as Jack slammed a shell into the chamber of the bolt-action rifle.

Chase released his clenched fist, letting the bull-whip drop to the floor.

"How'd you know I had a stash buried up here?" Jack asked.

"A hunch," Chase said. "You know how that is,

Jack." As he spoke, Chase noted the shattered glass on the floor of the shack, as if someone had thrown a bottle against the wall. A gaping hole in the shack's floorboards revealed a corroded metal box stuffed with paper money. Now where the hell would a dumb brute like Jack get all that filthy lucre? he wondered.

"As I recall," Chase said evenly, "you had fresh dirt on your boots the last time I hauled you in. Dust is one thing. Fresh dirt, that's another. That means somebody's done some digging."

"You're too smart for your own damn good, Beaudine." The rustler's voice cracked with edgy laughter. "Which is why I'm going to have to do something I'm already beginning to regret. I'm going to have to pump some lead into that skull of yours. Slow you down a little. Give us less fortunate folks a chance."

The tendons of Chase's neck stiffened as Jack spoke. The rustler might be dumb, but he was plenty vicious enough to commit cold-blooded murder. "You don't want a homicide rap on your hands, Jack. There's no percentage in that."

"Depends on who's doing the calculating. You see, what I don't want is to get caught again. I'm getting real sick of that. It's startin' to eat away at me."

As Jack began an embittered analysis of the various and sundry times that Chase had apprehended him, Chase himself came to an unsettling awareness. The information filtered back to him from the tension in his fists and the sledgehammer blows of his heart. It burned along his nerve endings, galvanizing his thoughts and awakening him to an insight so fundamental, he wondered why he'd never experienced it before. *He didn't want to die.* Not on this misty summer morning, and not for a very long time if he could arrange it.

It wasn't fear triggering the insight. He'd stared into the eyes of death plenty of times, but never with such a keen sense of needing to survive, of wanting to beat the odds. Now, with a gun at his back, he didn't have the time—or the inclination—to examine the reasons, he just knew there was something he had to keep breathing for. The future seemed to be beckoning to him, holding out some crazy promise of happiness.

It almost made him dizzy, that eerie feeling of destiny. He felt as if he'd been given a glimpse of his own fate. And on the heels of that realization came the unavoidable "reason" for his reawakening. A mental fanfare of trumpets announced her name: *Annie*.

He moaned. Annie? She was the reason he wanted to keep on breathing? The woman was his hanging judge, his jury. She'd made his life a living hell. But even as he tried to convince himself that she wasn't his manifest destiny, he could feel the truth crowding in on him, strangling all his objections.

Annie Wells was a bottle of bad liquor he couldn't keep corked, but God help him, he couldn't stand the thought of never seeing her again. He might as well be dead as live with that kind of emptiness.

A gun barrel nudged Chase's shoulder. "Beaudine? Are you listening to me?"

"So help me, God, I didn't hear a word you said, Jack. I was thinking about a woman."

"A woman? At a time like this? Hell, you *need* a bullet in the head."

Cold metal dug into the base of Chase's skull. The deadly soft click of the rifle's hammer exploded in his mind. He lashed back savagely with his bootheel, landing a blow to the rustler's shins. A shot rang out as Jack stumbled backward, firing wildly. Chase dropped, hitting the dust and grabbing for his whip at the same time. He wrapped the rawhide thong around Jack's legs so many times, Jack toppled like a piece of rotten timber.

"Looks like your streak is over," said Chase, scooping up the gun the rustler dropped and aiming it at his heaving chest. "I ought to be pissed at you, Jack. Hell, I ought to empty this rifle into your black heart . . . but I'm just not in the mood. Take a gander at me," Chase said, giving in to a roguish smile that would not be subdued. "You're looking at a man with a future, Jack, and that's the only blessed reason you're alive."

Chase swung off his horse, lifted the bullwhip from his saddle horn, and took the front steps of the cabin two at a time. "Annie? Where are you?" he called. She'd scared the hell out of him, disappearing from their campsite. Her horse was gone, too, which meant she'd probably come back to the cabin. Either that or she was lost somewhere in the hills.

Shadow followed on Chase's heels, barking excitedly as Chase entered the cabin and made a quick visual search of the area. There was no sign of her anywhere, and nothing to indicate that she'd been there. "Come on, boy," called Chase, motioning the dog with him as he headed out to check the barn.

But Shadow refused to follow. Whining excitedly, he urged Chase toward the bedroom. "Oh, God, not again," Chase said, spotting the open vault door. "Nobody falls in the same pit twice."

The lantern he'd taken off the kitchen wall flickered in Chase's grasp as he made his way down the tunnel. Annie's voice came to him, echoing faintly as he neared the cavern, but he couldn't make out the words. It sounded as if she was talking to herself, which relieved his mind, but only for a moment. What if she'd hit her head in the fall? What if she'd gone crazier than a loon?

"Annie?" He burst into the cavern, the lantern swinging wildly as he reached the pit. "Are you all right?"

The beam illuminated her surprised smile. "Chase!" she said, squinting up at him from the depths of the pit. "When did you get here? Johnny and I were just—"

"Are you all right?" He hesitated, registering what she'd said. "Johnny? Who—"

"Right here, buddy."

"Starhawk?" Chase held out the lantern, searching for the face to accompany the familiar voice. He nearly dropped the lantern into the pit as the angular features of a man he hadn't seen in five years materialized in the flow of light. "Starhawk? What are you doing here? What are you doing down there? With her?"

"He fell in the pit," Annie explained. "It's a long story, but I was trying to help him out. And I fell in too."

"This is some woman, Chase," Johnny said. "She's as gutsy as they come. Why have you been keeping her such a secret?"

Johnny's dark smile gave Chase a moment of true consternation. He might have been more pleased to see his long-lost partner if he hadn't known all about Johnny's heartbreaker reputation with women. Starhawk was half American Indian, and the renegade-with-a-cause image had worked miracles for him since he'd become a civilian, with both women and juries. A recent landmark Supreme Court decision in his favor had made him the hottest civil-rights lawyer in the country—as if members of the female sex needed any more provocation to fling themselves at his feet.

"Hang on," Chase said brusquely. "I'll get the ladder."

"No hurry," Johnny called back. "Annie and I were just discovering that we had some things in common."

"What does that mean?" Chase asked suspiciously.

"Nothing to get excited about. She likes spicy food, and so do I, that's all."

"You're sure? That's all?"

"Well, yeah, other than western novels. We both love those, don't we, Annie, and—"

"And what?"

"Chase!" Annie broke in, "could you get us out of this pit?"

"Not until I get an answer," Chase said. "And *what*?"

"You sure you want to know, Beaudine?"

"Spit it out, Starhawk."

"Okay, cowboy, but remember, you asked for it. Annie here tells me she likes men of the Indian persuasion. Says she was raised in a rain forest where the natives were as quick and agile as cats." Johnny's handsome face broke in a wide grin. "The lady has impeccable taste, Chase. If you're not going to marry her, I might. You ever notice her eyes? Amazing. I didn't know eyes came that blue."

"I've noticed." Chase thrust out the lantern, but not so he could get a look at Annie's eyes. He wanted to see her reaction to Starhawk's disgusting load of bull. Annie beamed up at him, blushing like a spring bride. Hell, the woman was glowing. She looked as if someone had hooked her up to an electrical power plant. "You forget, Johnny," Chase said, his voice deadly soft, "I'm already married to her."

Starhawk's smile broadened. "You forget, Chase. I'm a lawyer. I can have that marriage annulled."

"Too late for that, my friend. The union's been consummated. Annie and I slept together last night."

"Chase!" Annie's eyes flashed a warning. "That's getting a little personal, don't you think? Now please get us out of here!"

Her tone brooked no more nonsense, but Chase wasn't anywhere near through with Johnny Starhawk. He went for the ladder, and once he had them both out of the pit, he resumed the sparring match with his ex-partner. "Starhawk on marriage?" Chase shot at Johnny. "That's a ripe one. You're incapable of committing to a relationship. You'd make a good woman miserable."

"You already have, Beaudine," Johnny cut back, with a meaningful glance at Annie.

Chase's eyes flared with violence that was barely in check. His voice dropped low, obscenely calm. "Let's finish this conversation outside," he said. "Just you and me, Starhawk."

Annie caught her breath. She'd seen Chase kill a man in Costa Brava, but she'd never seen him look more deadly than at this moment. The blunt force of his anger swept the room, stunning her to silence.

He was demonically dark, breathtaking. *But someone was going to get hurt*, she realized.

Johnny responded to Chase's challenge with a slow nod.

"No!" Annie cried. "That's enough, you two! I'm not going to marry either one of you, is that clear? And I don't appreciate being a trophy to be won by the fastest gun."

"Stay out of this, Annie." As Chase pulled off his denim jacket, tossing aside the coat, a sizable chunk of bluish glass flew out of his pocket and landed at Annie's feet.

Annie knelt to pick up the glass, noting the whitish coating and medicinal smell. On the other side of the glass, a small section of the label still remained. "Chase!" she said, rising. "Where did you get this?"

"Why?"

"It's the same antacid the foreman bought in the drugstore."

"What are you talking about?" Chase stopped in the process of rolling up his sleeves. He stared at Annie hard, putting his wrath on hold for an instant. "What foreman?"

Annie quickly recounted the story about meeting the foreman from the McAffrey ranch and giving him some tips about natural medicine. "He didn't take my advice," she observed.

Chase took the glass from Annie, examining it. "He was swigging this stuff in the Prairie Oyster Tavern." Chase's focus shot inward as he stared at the glass, as though he was thinking hard and fast, putting things together. "That S.O.B.," he said under his breath. "He's been paying Jack to be a decoy, to throw me off the track while he loots his own ranch—and everybody else's."

"Who?" Annie asked.

"Yeah, who?" Johnny echoed.

"The McAffreys' foreman," said Chase, still fixated on the glass. "He must have been meeting Jack up at the shack, paying him off. He was probably behind the jailbreak too."

"Really?" Annie was fascinated. "The foreman's been rustling cattle from his own ranch? Just like in the book I read?"

"Not exactly," Chase said. "He's been hiring 'ranch hands' to do his dirty work for him. But he's the mastermind, I'd bet my life on it." Chase dropped the piece of glass in his shirt pocket, scooped up his denim jacket, and grabbed a rifle off the wall. A look of total and savage concentration crossed his features.

"Hey!" said Annie, watching him stride toward the door. "Where are you going?"

"To get that bastard," Chase said bluntly. "He's been screwing with me for weeks. Now I'm going to screw him—right into the ground."

"All right!" Johnny's voice was husky with laughter as he joined Chase. "Let's kick some butt. I'll go with you, buddy. You may need backup."

Annie stood there, astonished as the two men broke into grins and slapped hands in some sort of male ritual. A moment later they were heading out the door as though they'd forgotten she was there. Or had ever been there!

It was their macho laughter that galvanized Annie into action. Not two minutes ago they'd been fighting over her! Now she could hear them outside, loading rifles, trading war stories, and whatever other silly things males did when they were planning to "kick butt."

She noticed Chase's bullwhip lying on the cot where he'd left it, apparently forgotten in his haste. She remembered vividly the times he'd used the ghastly thing on her. Had anyone ever used it on him? she wondered.

The two men were getting into the Bronco when Annie stepped out onto the front porch. "Chase Beaudine!" she called out, whip in hand. "Don't you dare get into that car."

Chase glanced up, his dark eyes shadowed by his Stetson. "Annie? What are you doing?"

"Whatever I have to," she said, shaking the whip

out as though she fully intended to use it. "You're not going anywhere, cowboy. Not until I'm through with you."

Johnny let out a soft war whoop. "She sounds serious."

"Annie, be reasonable," Chase said. "I've got a rustler to deal with here—"

"No, you've got a woman to deal with. *Here*. That foreman isn't going anywhere. He can wait. I can't."

"Beaudine!" Johnny let out a howl of rich laughter. "You didn't tell me she could crack the whip! I'm in love."

Annie's head was not turned by the flattery. She addressed Chase's ex-partner politely, her voice steely-soft. "Johnny, it's been wonderful meeting you again after all these years, but would you please leave? Chase and I have some talking to do."

Neither man moved immediately, so Annie descended the steps into the open, the whip slithering behind her as she took a stand, facing Chase. Her hand began to shake as she drew the rawhide thong up, getting the feel of it. She had no idea whether she could actually throw a whip or not, but she'd learned from observing the best, Chase himself. Every nuance of his prowess with the terrifying weapon, even his slightest muscle twitch, was recorded indelibly in her mind.

Chase marveled as he watched Annie struggle with the bullwhip. It reared up, dipping and bobbing like a drunken snake as she tried to throw it, and then it dropped to the ground with a limp shudder. Swearing a blue streak, she kept at it until the snake began to sober up a little.

Chase bit back a smile. She looked like Calamity Jane having a bad day. At the rate she was going, it would take her till Christmas, but his heart went out to her. The whip was almost three times her size, and he knew she was scared to death of it. She must have been in a hell-hot fury even to touch the thing.

"Annie, put it down," he said finally, approaching her. "Somebody could get hur—" But before he could get the last word out, before he could even blink his astonished eyes, the rawhide thong arced up and flashed at him like a lightning strike, snapping the Stetson clean off his head.

"Hot damn," Johnny whispered.

Chase's heart kicked like a vicious rodeo bronc. He raked a hand through his dark hair in astonishment, unable to believe what she'd done. She could have taken his eye out! He wanted to be angry with her, but it wasn't possible. The stunned admiration he felt didn't leave room for any other emotion. Her features were ablaze with a triumphant smile, her eyes crackling with hot blue excitement. She was truly the damnedest, sexiest woman he'd ever known.

"Get the hell out of here, would you, Johnny?" Chase said. "I've got a woman to deal with."

"Lucky dog." Johnny chuckled softly as he headed for a crimson Ferrari Testarossa parked off the road. As he reached the gleaming car, he called back, "I'll be in town at the hotel if you need me, Chase. Be gentle with him, Annie."

Johnny was gone in a cloud of pale dust, leaving Annie and Chase to stand there under the sweltering Wyoming sun, taking each other's measure. Annie felt a surge of sweet terror as she witnessed the whipcrack of desire in Chase's eyes. *Dark lightning,* she thought. The man looked as though he meant to have her right there on the grass.

He started toward her, and she yanked back the whip, menacing him. "Back it up, cowboy," she said. "You're not getting near me until I get some answers."

"Annie, I don't give one sweet damn about catching rustlers at the moment. Is that what you wanted to hear? All I want is you, Angel, flat on your back and spread-eagled, hotter than hell and wanting me back."

"Chase! Stop that!" She backed up, a bubble of startled laughter betraying her outrage. "You're not touching me until you explain yourself! I don't give a damn about rustlers either. I want to know why you said those things to Johnny. About being married to me, and the union being consummated?"

"Well, we are married." His rugged features drifted into a sensual smile as he realized where her concerns lay. "And we did consummate . . . last night. You haven't forgotten how we finally managed that, have you, Annie? I know I never will."

He hooked his thumbs in his belt loops, which drew his snug jeans even lower than usual on his hips. It was a blatantly sexy move, and had the effect of reminding Annie exactly how they'd managed to consummate, down to the last embarrassing detail. If he was playing games with her, he was an incredibly cruel man.

"You heard me, Beaudine," she warned softly, fiercely. "Explain yourself. Last night you wanted nothing whatsoever to do with marriage, screaming brats, or yellow curtains, remember?"

Chase drew in a deep breath, as though to settle things down and get control of the situation. He straightened his collar and combed a hand through his hair, making its dark wildness a little more presentable. "I'm saying I'll honor the marriage if that's what you want," he told her. "I'll go to the immigration people, and tell them I married you in Costa Brava. I'm saying it's official, Annie. You're my wife."

Listening to him, Annie had a sensation of lightness that swept her whole body. She thought her heart was going to float right out of her chest. There was just one thing keeping her planted on the ground. His choice of words. *It's official?* That was much too sterile a reference for Annie. She couldn't imagine why he'd used a phrase like that . . . unless it was his conscience talking. What had he done? Spent all night convincing himself to do the right thing by her?

"I don't want sacrifices from you, Chase. I might have accepted that offer the day I came here, but not now. Too much has happened."

Chase didn't know whether to laugh or cry at the irony of the situation. The tables had been turned.

Last night he'd been questioning her motives. Now she didn't trust his. Somehow he had to make her understand what he hadn't understood himself, that he'd been opened up last night, first by the physical act of love, and then by the brush with death. He'd been opened up by knowing her.

"I'm not sacrificing anything, Annie. I've been winking at death all my life. Maybe that was the only thing that made me feel alive. But I've got a better reason to draw breath now. We're married—and I want it that way."

"You do? *Why?*"

That was the question. He and Annie Wells were total opposites. They went at things completely differently. There were a dozen contradictions in her nature, but there was one underlying truth at the heart of her. She was a willow, unconquerably strong, surrendering gracefully to the inevitable. Whereas he was as rigid as a giant blue oak. But he was learning. Learning how to lose the fight and win the war, learning how to love a woman.

"I can't put it into words," he told her, "not the exact words anyway. I know a woman likes to hear how a man's out-of-his-head in love and can't live without her. And all that's true enough in my case, but it's not the reason. It's something much simpler, and not very poetic."

He heaved a sigh, trying to find words for something that couldn't be explained. "I feel better about myself when I'm around you, Annie. I just do. Oh, I know that's hard to believe the way I've been acting lately. But it's there, inside me." His voice gave way on him, cracking as he added, "Something that's never been there before."

"Chase . . ."

"I love you, Annie."

Annie choked back a quaver of wild disbelief, of joy. She was too shocked to move, too shaken, which was probably all right, because she never would have made it over to where he stood. Suddenly he was miles away, and a huge, impassible chasm seemed to separate them. It was a chasm created by her own astonished heart. She'd wanted this so long, so badly, she simply couldn't believe it was happening.

"Come here, Annie," he said, holding out his arms.

Tears blurred her vision as she felt the irresistible tug of his husky voice. She could remember so clearly her prophecy of what would happen if he ever said those words to her. She would go to him. She wouldn't have any choice. He would own her, body and soul.

"Oh, God, Chase." She closed her eyes, unaccountably frightened as she tried to find the means to move. The more she fought the strange paralysis, the more her arms seemed anchored at her sides, her legs weighted down. And suddenly he was there, dragging her into his arms, a harsh groan on his lips. He had come to her.

She flung her arms around his neck with a sob of relief. Tears stung her eyes as she surrendered to the rough passion of his embrace, thrilling to the way he lifted her off her feet in a fierce hug.

He settled her back on the ground and brought her head up, his eyes probing her mind, her heart, sinking to the depths of her soul. "Do you still want to be my wife, Annie? Will you marry me? Again?"

The answer swept into Annie's mind on a peal of bells so clamorous, it probably reverberated throughout the known universe. But when she opened her mouth to speak, nothing came out except a hoarse squeak of emotion.

"Was that a yes, Annie? Because, to be honest with you, I don't have a whole lot to give a woman." He caught hold of her hand, bringing it up in the traditional style of a man about to put a ring on a woman's finger. Instead, he drew something from his shirt pocket and settled it gently into her cupped palm. "But I can promise you this. There will always be flowers."

Annie looked down at the daisy he'd placed in her hand, a new and perfect flower to replace the one long dead that he'd "picked" for her with his whip. Something unbearably sweet flared through her senses, making it impossible to tell him how much she loved the flower, how terribly she loved him.

She brought the daisy to her lips, tears in her eyes. "It's enough," she said.

Epilogue

It was a summer morning too perfect for anything but the quiet celebration of nature, picking wild blackberries on the banks of a lazy mountain river . . . or marrying the man you adore alongside it. Annie chose the latter, and she had never looked more lovely. Her wedding gown was a simple white organdy, its sweetheart neckline revealing soft, rounded shoulders and porcelain skin, glowing with excitement. A garland of wild daisies adorned her copper-colored hair.

Chase wore a chamois jacket with western fringe swinging from the sleeves; a brand-new black Stetson shaded his dark eyes in honor of the occasion. Several of the women in the small assemblage of guests regarded him with frankly admiring glances as he stood before the preacher, waiting for his bride. And Muriel Jensen, who sang the Lord's Prayer, was overheard referring to the groom as "outlandishly handsome."

The crowd hushed as Annie came forward to join Chase. Even the finches' throaty chirping in the willows overhead went quiet as the bride took her place next to the groom. Anticipation peaked as the couple's eyes met for one sweet, brief moment before they turned to face the priest. And then someone released a sigh.

Johnny Starhawk was Chase's best man, his dark hair tied back, his expression solemn as the nuptials began. Next to Johnny sat Chase's Border collie, his tail thumping noisily. The melodious rush of the river provided background music for the short ceremony, but as the priest pronounced the couple husband and wife, and they sealed their union with a lingering kiss, an odd rumbling noise could be heard in the distance.

As Annie and Chase finally turned to the crowd, the ominous sound built, roaring like a fleet of approaching helicopters. The earth seemed to vibrate, and the racket soared to a crescendo as a single streak of black and chrome burst into view. To everyone's surprise, a huge motorcycle swooped around the bend in the road that led to the river.

"Who is he?" Voices in the crowd rose anxiously as a lone figure on a massive black Harley shot straight for the ceremony. The rider's mirrored aviator glasses flashed in the sunlight, and the ties of the black bandanna he wore around his head streamed in the wind.

The rider looked as menacing as the demon machine he rode as he gunned the bike up onto the grass and wheeled it around, coming to a stop not six feet from the startled crowd. Sunlight glinted off his glasses as he scanned their faces, searching for someone. Unshorn and unshaven, his rich blond hair sun-whitened against the black bandanna, he was a blunt weapon to the senses. A golden mountain lion of a man.

Both Chase and Johnny seemed to recognize the rider as he dropped the bike's kickstand and swung off. But it was Annie who said the man's name. In his marine fatigues, olive-drab T-shirt, and flak vest, Geoff Dias looked exactly as Annie remembered him from five years before. He was a stark and beautiful specter from the past, reminding her of every tragic detail, every shining moment, of the commandos' last mission.

She glanced at Chase beside her and realized that

he was remembering it, too, every moment, as though time had turned in on itself and rushed backward. Even Johnny Starhawk looked oddly transfixed.

"Chase Beaudine?" said Geoff, approaching the gathering. "I was told I could find him here." The crowd inched back as if the stranger really were a mountain lion.

Chase made a path through the throng, drawing Annie behind him. "Dias! It's me, Chase."

Geoff Dias stared at Chase's wedding apparel in total confusion. "What's going on, Beaudine? I got an urgent message. It said your life was in danger."

"Sorry, buddy," Chase informed him, a slow smile breaking. "You're too late to save me now. I just got married."

"Married?" Geoff's rugged features registered shock as he stared at his old friend. "I don't believe it. Chase Beaudine married?" Husky laughter erupted, and he shook his head in disbelief. "God, man, I'm really sorry to hear that. Maybe if I'd been here an hour earlier, I could have saved you."

"If you'd been here an hour earlier, you could have given away the bride." The sardonic remark came from Johnny Starhawk as he moved through the crowd to greet the late arrival.

"Starhawk? What are you doing here?"

Johnny grinned, his dark eyes glinting as he clasped hands with his former partner. "Part of the conspiracy to get Chase Beaudine out of action."

Geoff Dias glanced again at Chase, now wholly sympathetic to the man's plight. "When you said you were in danger, Beaudine, you meant it!"

"Maybe you'd like to meet the danger in person." Chase ushered Annie forward, draping an arm around her shoulder. "This is my beautiful wife. You may remember her as Annie Wells."

Recognition slowly crept into Geoff's emerald green eyes as he searched Annie's luminous face. "She's the girl you rescued," he said finally. "The one they told us was dead." He turned to Chase with new understanding. "She's more than beautiful, Beaudine. She's eerie. No wonder you lost your head."

Annie reached out her hand and caught hold of Geoff's. "Thank you," she said, her eyes going misty, and very, very blue. A moment later Geoff pulled her into his arms.

It was a friendly enough welcome, but Chase broke them up anyway, drawing his tiny wife away from Geoff Dias's bear hug of an embrace. "Find your own woman, Dias," he said possessively, enfolding Annie in his arms. "This one's mine."

The other two men stepped back, laughing at their old friend's uncharacteristic behavior.

"Don't be so smug, compadres," Chase warned them both. "It could happen to you."

Both Chase and Annie laughed at the men's vehement denials. But as Annie studied her husband's former partners, a stirring of intuition warned her that these two men *were* inveterate loners, and probably as averse to emotional involvement as Chase had been. She didn't envy the woman who tangled with either of them. As for Geoff Dias, she would not want to be the woman who tried to tame that lion. It would surely take a whip and a chair. Or one very smart lioness.

And as for Johnny Starhawk, he was as quietly dangerous as any jungle cat she'd ever come across, a black panther lying in wait. But for whom? If she could have looked into the future and seen the unsuspecting one who would cross his path, Annie would have warned her to run for her life.

She gave an involuntary shudder, grateful to be exactly where she was, warm in Chase's arms. Laughing voices rose and champagne corks began to pop in the background, bringing her back to the celebration at hand—her own wedding! Glancing up at the love in her husband's dark eyes, at her most secret dream realized, she joined in the joyous laughter. Miracle Number Two, she thought. *May there be many more.*

THE EDITOR'S CORNER

Next month LOVESWEPT brings you spirited heroines and to-die-for heroes in stories that explore romance in all its forms—sensuous, sweet, heartwarming, and funny. And the title of each novel is so deliciously compelling, you won't know which one to read first.

There's no better way to describe Gavin Magadan than as a **LEAN MEAN LOVING MACHINE,** LOVESWEPT #546, by Sandra Chastain, for in his boots and tight jeans he is one dangerously handsome hunk. And Stacy Lanham has made a bet to vamp him! How can she play the seducer when she's much better at replacing spark plugs than setting off sparks? Gavin shows her the way, though, when he lets himself be charmed by the lady whose lips he yearns to kiss. Sandra has created a winner with this enthralling story.

In **SLOW BURN,** LOVESWEPT #547, by Cindy Gerard, passion heats to a boiling point between Joanna Taylor and Adam Dursky. When he takes on the job of handyman in her lodge, she's drawn to a loneliness in him that echoes her own, and she longs for his strong embrace with a fierce desire. Can a redheaded rebel who's given up on love heal the pain of a tough renegade? The intensity of Cindy's writing makes this a richly emotional tale you'll long remember.

In Linda Jenkins's newest LOVESWEPT, #548, Sam Wonder *is* **MR. WONDERFUL,** a heart-stopping combination of muscles and cool sophistication. But he's furious when Trina Bartok shows up at his Ozarks resort, convinced she's just the latest candidate in his father's endless matchmaking. Still, he can't deny the sensual current that crackles between them, and when Trina makes it clear she's there only for a temporary job, he resolves to make her a permanent part of his life. Be sure not to miss this treat from Linda.

Judy Gill's offering for the month, **SUMMER LOVER,** LOVESWEPT #549, will have you thinking summer may be the most romantic season of all—although romance is the furthest thing from Donna Mailer's mind when she goes to Gray Kincaid's office to refuse his offer to buy her uncle's failing campground business. After all, the Kincaid family nearly ruined her life. But Gray's passionate persuasion soon has her sweetly surrendering amid tangled sheets. Judy's handling of this story is nothing less than superb.

Most LOVESWEPTs end with the hero and heroine happily deciding to marry, but Olivia Rupprecht, who has quickly developed a reputation for daring to be different, begins **I DO!,** #550, with Sol Standish in the Middle East and Mariah Garnett in the Midwest exchanging wedding vows through the telephone—and that's before they ever lay eyes on each other. When they finally come face-to-face, will their innocent love survive the test of harsh reality? Olivia will take your breath away with this original and stunning romance.

INTIMATE VIEW by Diane Pershing, LOVESWEPT #551, will send you flying in a whirlwind of exquisite sensation. Ben Kane certainly feels that way when he glimpses a goddess rising naked from the ocean. He resented being in a small California town to run a cable franchise until he sees Nell Pritchard and she fires his blood—enough to make him risk the danger of pursuing the solitary spitfire whose sanctuary he's invaded. Diane's second LOVESWEPT proves she's one of the finest newcomers to the genre.

On sale this month from FANFARE are three marvelous novels. The historical romance **HEATHER AND VELVET** showcases the exciting talent of a rising star—Teresa Medeiros. Her marvelous touch for creating memorable characters and her exquisite feel for portraying passion and emotion shine in this grand adventure of love between a bookish orphan and a notorious highwayman known as the Dreadful Scot Bandit. Ranging from the storm-swept English countryside to the wild moors of Scotland, **HEATHER AND VELVET** has garnered the following praise from *New York Times* bestselling author Amanda Quick: "A terrific tale full of larger-than-life characters and thrilling romance." Teresa Medeiros—a name to watch for.

Lush, dramatic, and poignant, **LADY HELLFIRE,** by Suzanne Robinson, is an immensely thrilling historical romance. Its hero, Alexis de Granville, Marquess of Richfield, is a cold-blooded rogue whose tragic—and possibly violent—past has hardened his heart to love . . . until he melts at the fiery touch of Kate Grey's sensual embrace.

Anna Eberhardt, whose short romances have been published under the pseudonym Tiffany White, has been nominated for *Romantic Times*'s Career Achievement award for Most Sensual Romance in a series. Now she delivers **WHISPERED HEAT,** a compelling contemporary novel of love lost, then regained. When Slader Reems is freed after five years of being wrongly imprisoned, he sets out to reclaim everything that was taken from him—including Lissa Jamison.

Also on sale this month, in the Doubleday hardcover edition, is **LIGHTNING,** by critically acclaimed Patricia Potter. During the Civil War, nobody was a better Confederate blockade runner than Englishman Adrian Cabot, but Lauren Bradley swore to stop him. Together they would be swept into passion's treacherous sea, tasting deeply of ecstasy and the danger of war.

Happy reading!

With warmest wishes,

Nita Taublib
Associate Publisher
LOVESWEPT and FANFARE

✿   ✿   ✿   ✿   ✿

From the Bestselling Author of
THE MORGAN WOMEN
and THE FLAMES OF VENGEANCE

THE FIREBIRDS
by Beverly Byrne

*A glorious, sweeping novel of passionate intrigue, romantic mystery,
and a proud woman's passion for truth.*

They were bound by a centuries-old conspiracy of secrecy and
scandal . . . generations of the mighty Mendozas have conquered
persecution and treachery to become one of the world's most powerful families. Now one valiant woman seeks the truth of her
heritage . . . and threatens to destroy them all.

England 1939
Murder shatters the peace of the countryside, and a beautiful society
matron disappears without a trace. Few know that behind the shock-
ing crime stands the House of Mendoza . . . a secret the rulers of
the dynasty are sworn to protect.

London 1970
An indomitable young woman seeks to rip aside the curtain that
obscures her past. Armed only with her wits and her desperate need
to know, clever and courageous Lili Cramer pits herself against the
power of the Mendozas and finds terror, truth . . . and a love she
will never forget.

New York 1980
A man learns that he can close his mind to the sins of his family, but he
cannot erase the memory of the only woman who has ever touched his
heart.

From the hot and hectic streets of New York, to the cool and gracious
manors of the English aristocracy, to the sun-drenched palaces of

southern Spain . . . echoes of the past ignite a blaze in the present. Only the Firebirds can rise triumphant from the ashes.

Prologue

England: 1939

At a few minutes past two P.M. on the seventh of April, a single ray of sunlight glimmered on the sodden earth of a rainswept garden in Sussex. Lady Swanning tipped her extremely pretty young face upward and felt the welcome warmth. At that moment she heard the first cuckoo of spring.

The bird's distinctive call echoed in the stillness of the garden. It was Good Friday, and most of the staff of the great house had been released from their duties for the afternoon. Lady Swanning and the bird had the far-flung lawns and the beds of tender spring flowers entirely to themselves.

She thought about the cuckoo. Somewhere it would find the nest of another bird and deposit one of its eggs. When the hatchlings emerged, the cuckoo baby would destroy the rightful children, either by pecking them to death or pushing them to the ground. The conscripted foster parents, unaware of how they'd been duped, would nurture the changeling. Lady Swanning believed the cuckoo was a marvelously clever creature.

The sunlight faded and another bank of clouds rolled across the Sussex downs. Lady Swanning glanced at her elegant gold watch. Two-thirty, almost time. Casting a last look at the garden, she began walking toward the great stone house built centuries before.

How sad that she must leave all this. She had loved her life since marriage, adored the excitement of race meetings and dinner parties and balls, thrived on being the feted and admired young wife of Emery Preston-Wilde, the thirteenth Viscount Swanning.

Regret did not alter her decision.

As she had anticipated, the servants had left for church and the house was hushed and still. Lady Swanning and her husband were also expected to attend the service. Emery was to read one of the lessons, as his forebears had done for generations. This year would be different, for reasons which only Lady Swanning understood.

In the gun room she quickly found what she wanted, a Mauser that Emery had appropriated from a German officer in the Great War. Like all her husband's guns, the pistol was oiled and ready. To become a lethal weapon it had only to be loaded with the cartridges kept in a locked drawer in the sixteenth-century Jacobean cabinet. The night before, while Emery slept, she'd taken the key. It had been quite simple.

Loaded now, the small snub-nosed pistol fit easily into the pocket of her tweed jacket. Lady Swanning returned to the long corridor, her footsteps making no sound on the Oriental carpet. Moments later she stood before the study door and looked again at her watch. It was two forty-five.

"I'll be in my study," her husband had said at lunch. "Meet me there and we'll go on to church. Say, quarter to three?" He'd looked up from his poached salmon. "Do try for once to be on time, my dear."

She was exactly on time. Lady Swanning smiled, then went in. Emery stood with his back to her, staring out the tall French doors that led to a walled rose garden. He was a big man. His form blotted out much of the gray light. "Damned rain's starting again," he said without looking around.

"Yes." She took the pistol from her pocket and thumbed off the safety catch. It made only the tiniest sound.

"Well, nothing for it, we have to go."

"No," she said quietly. "I don't think so. Not today."

"Don't be silly. There's no way we can—" He turned, an expression of annoyance on his face. Then he saw the gun. "What are you doing with that?"

She didn't answer. It seemed to her unnecessary since her intention must be obvious.

The cook, the parlor maid, the chauffeur, and her ladyship's social secretary were the skeleton staff in the house that afternoon. At five minutes to three the cook and the maid heard two explosive noises and ran to the study. They found Lord Swanning lying facedown in a pool of blood. Their first impression was that he'd fallen and injured himself. The cook struggled to roll the viscount over. That's when she saw his staring eyes and the gaping, bloody wound in his chest and began to scream.

The chauffeur and the secretary arrived within moments, summoned by the screams, though both subsequently denied hearing the shots.

Lady Swanning was nowhere to be found. The police looked long and hard—until a few months later when war broke out and diverted them—but she seemed to have vanished from the earth.

* * * * *

FORTUNE'S CHILD
by Pamela Simpson

Twenty years ago, Christina Fortune disappeared. Now she's come home to claim what's rightfully hers. But is she an heiress . . . or an imposter?

She was a woman of ambitious dreams

Other women had claimed to be Christina Fortune, missing heiress to one of the world's largest shipping empires. Now this beautiful, self-assured woman had stepped out of the shadows of the past, daring to take what she insisted was hers.

She was a woman of mystery

Her heart was tormented by yesterday's secrets. What happened twenty years ago to drive a sheltered fifteen-year-old away from her privileged life, her wealthy family, and into the dark and dangerous city streets? Where had Christina gone? And what was she running from?

She was a woman of fortune

She had promises to keep—to the girl she once was, and to another. Now, from San Francisco to Hawaii to exotic Hong Kong, she must fight to gain control of the family business, fight to convince them all that she is Christina. But the hardest fight of all will be against her own blossoming desire . . . for a man she dares not trust, a man who has too much to lose if she is who she claims.

Christina looked around her at the lush coconut palm grove that dotted the crescent-shaped, white sand beach; the small, shallow lagoon; the massive stone wall formed from lava that once flowed here; and a tall, narrow, thatched building.

"Pu'uhonua," she whispered. Then, looking at Ross, she translated, "It means *place of refuge.*"

"Do you remember it?" Ross asked, watching her carefully.

She knew perfectly well what he meant. "My parents used to bring me here on picnics, when I was little. I thought it was a wonderful place to swim. It was only when I was older that I understood the significance of it."

"And what is that?"

She was sure that he knew as much about this place as she did. "It's a sacred refuge, the ancient home of an *ali'i*, a ruling chief. Defeated warriors could take refuge here and their enemies couldn't harm them. People who had broken the *kapu* came here. The Hawaiians believed that breaking the sacred *kapu* offended the gods and the gods would react by causing lava flows, tidal waves or earthquakes. So if someone broke the *kapu*, he would be pursued and killed, unless he could reach this place."

Ross knew about the ancient legend, but he found himself drawn to the way she explained it with almost childlike wonder. "And if he made it here?" he prompted.

"A ceremony of absolution was performed by the *kahuna pule*, the priest, and all was forgiven. This was a place of life, where someone could find a second chance." Once again there was that faint wistfulness in her voice, that hinted at more than she wanted to reveal.

"Second chances," Ross repeated thoughtfully. He stood near the water's edge, his back to the small lagoon, the breeze lifting his hair from his forehead. He almost looked like an *ali'i* himself, with his black hair, dark skin, and air of command. Christina could easily imagine him presiding over a kingdom like this, just as he presided over the kingdom that was Fortune International.

At that moment she understood perfectly why Katherine had chosen him over everyone else to run the company. He had the steely determination, confidence, and strength that was needed to run a multi-national company like Fortune International, and to fight Richard Fortune and anyone else who attempted to take it away from Katherine. She knew he would fight her with equal determination. Suddenly she was frightened of him, and it was all she could do not to tremble before his relentless, probing gaze.

He asked, "If you really are Christina Fortune, is that why you came back? For a second chance?"

She was caught off guard by the question. It was far more perceptive than Ross could possibly imagine, and for once her defenses weren't strong enough to hide the turbulent emotions beneath the carefully controlled surface.

"I . . ." She stopped, then looked away, focusing on the *ki'i*—a stone carving standing on a rock in the shallow end of the lagoon—, the Great Wall that had once separated the palace grounds from the commoners' huts, the temple itself, *anything* other than Ross.

He persisted, "Did you come to San Francisco looking for some kind of sanctuary?"

Her thoughts went back twenty years, to that terrifying night when two young girls had tried desperately to find a safe place, not only from the man who chased them but from the shared nightmare experience that had driven them to the dangerous streets of New York.

"I don't believe that sanctuary exists anywhere," she whispered. "Not even here at *Pu'uhonua*."

"What about forgiveness?"

Still not meeting his look, she said in a small voice, "That seems to be the most elusive thing of all."

She forced herself to look at him. There was a poignant expression in his eyes that revealed a vulnerability she never would have suspected he possessed. She was surprised to see that his own defenses were a bit shaky at that moment.

"How do *you* feel about forgiveness?" she asked. She was

uncertain exactly why the question had occurred to her, but as soon as she asked it, she knew she'd touched a nerve.

Anger glinted in those deep blue eyes. "As a virtue, I think it's highly overrated. Revenge makes a lot more sense to me than forgiveness."

"Then we have something in common."

Before he could question her further, she said, "I've had enough of interrogations for a while. I'm going swimming."

Turning her back on him, she pulled off the shorts and tank top, letting them fall on the sand, and kicked off her sandals. She was aware that he watched her as she raced into the water, splashing in the shallows, then throwing herself into the deeper part. The water was placid in the sheltered cove, with no breaking waves to impede her progress. With quick, sure strokes, she headed away from the beach, away from Ross and his disturbing questions and his even more disturbing presence.

She was careful not to swim out too far. She knew the current beyond the cove could be treacherous, and could easily carry her out to sea if she went too far. Gradually, she felt her body relax as the tension of their confrontation left her. The water was warm and clear. Beneath her, she could see schools of brightly-colored tropical fish swimming amid multi-colored coral. Turning around to face the beach, she treaded water and looked at the magnificent setting. Despite what she'd told Ross about sanctuary not existing anywhere, she felt drawn to this place. If there were such a thing as sanctuary, it would be here, in this lovely, serene setting.

Perhaps someday, if she accomplished what she'd set out to do, she could return here and try to find the forgiveness that had eluded her for twenty years, that had kept her heartsick in a way that nothing could alleviate.

Perhaps.

She saw Ross sitting on the beach, watching her. Her arms and legs were tired now, and she decided to return to the beach. But as she swam toward Ross, who stood there, waiting for her, she wasn't at all certain if she was swimming toward sanctuary—or danger.

SEASON OF SHADOWS

by Mary Mackey

author of A GRAND PASSION and
THE KINDNESS OF STRANGERS

*A spellbinding and intimately wrought story of love and friendship,
passion and purpose, revenge and redemption, and of the choices that
irrevocably alter a woman's life.*

Lucy and Cassandra were polar opposites: light and dark, pretty and
plain, cautious and wildly impulsive. But from the first day they met at
a Colorado prep school, Lucy and Cassie became the best of friends.
Roommates at Radcliffe during the turbulent sixties, they stood by
each other as Cassie seduced the man of her dreams and Lucy
succumbed to David, the fiery poet who broke her heart. When
beautiful blond Lucy meets Mila, the dashing crown prince of Patan,
she must decide if she can learn to love a man who promises her
everything, even though she has never forgotten David.

It was April, and outside Adams House the chestnut trees
were in bloom. Inside, Lucy and Mila sat naked on Mila's new
bed, their arms wrapped around one another, listening to sitar
music. The music flowed up and down invisible hills, tracing a
distant geography that seemed both remote and wonderful.
Mila's body, too, was a path into mysterious places. Lucy
rested against his shoulder, feeling warm and safe and more or
less at peace with the universe. Mila was an amazing man: he
knew more about loving than she had ever imagined a man
could know, and yet, at the same time he was her companion
and her friend and she grew closer to him every day.

The music stopped, leaving resonances in the air; the candle
sputtered and flickered; when the silence was perfect again,

Mila rose to his feet, crossed the room, and opened the closet door. Bending forward, he became part of the shadows; the muscles in his back rippled like the muscles of a dancer. He straightened up, turned, and walked back toward Lucy holding a small white box. The box was ivory, inlaid with gold. On the sides and lid, Patanese court ladies from another century sat beside a pool filled with swans and lotus blossoms.

"For you," he said, placing the box in her hands.

She examined it in wonder. Every detail was perfect, right down to the tiny feet of the ladies and the sharp beaks of the swans. She'd never seen anything so finely made. She turned the box over and discovered the small red seal of the artist stamped on the bottom: two fish swimming under a quarter moon. "Thank you," she said softly, awed by its perfection. "I don't know what to say. It's absolutely beautiful."

Mila sat down beside her and ran his finger over the lid of the box. "I'm glad you like it." He smiled. "It belonged to my mother."

"Are you sure you want to part with it?"

"Open it," he suggested.

She lifted the lid and there, lying on a pillow of blue satin, was a diamond necklace. Matched perfectly, the strands of diamonds sparkled like a chain of fire. "My God," she gasped, "you can't be serious. I couldn't possibly accept a present like this."

Mila picked up the necklace, held it for a moment in the palm of his hand, and then fastened it around her neck. The diamonds were cold on her bare skin, and she shivered as they touched the base of her throat.

"Marry me," he said. He put one finger over her lips. "No, don't tell me you can't because I'm a prince and you're a commoner. That sort of prejudice is ridiculous; it belongs to another world, one that died centuries ago. I am not going to let my family select a wife for me. I have learned here in

America that love is completely democratic; love doesn't care about money or social class or what other people will say. I'm speaking from my heart, and I'd say the same thing if I was the poorest peasant: I love you, Lucy. Marry me, and I'll do my best to make you happy."

She stared at the fire in his eyes and the pleading in his face, and she thought a hundred thoughts, none of them coherent. For the first time in her life she had the sense of being on the edge of some kind of destiny greater than herself, and it frightened her. She loved him, she didn't doubt that any longer, but when she tried to imagine herself leaving her own country to live in Patan, she felt a chill of alienation. She couldn't see herself as a princess. The idea of wearing a crown seemed almost laughable, like something out of a child's storybook. And there was something else, something she hated to admit even to herself: she still loved David. She didn't want to, but she did; David was buried in her flesh like a fish hook, snarled around her soul, and she kept trying to struggle free and never quite succeeding. It wouldn't be fair to Mila if she married him and only give him part of herself. She felt a long pang of regret; she loved Mila in so many ways, but not enough . . . "I'm sorry," she stuttered. She reached up to take off the necklace, but the clasp seemed stuck and her fingers didn't work right. "I can't marry you. It's not possible."

"Why not?" Mila's face changed suddenly as if a cloud had passed across it.

"Because," she paused, looking for words to soften the blow, "because even though I love you, I don't love you . . . enough to marry you."

"Is that the only reason?"

"Yes," she whispered. "I'm so terribly sorry."

To her surprise he looked relieved. "But you like me, yes?"

"Of course I like you, Mila. You and Cassie are my best friends in the world." She felt terrible. Her eyes burned with tears.

He took her hand in his and held it for a moment and there was a long silence. "In my country," he said at last, "we believe that liking is what is important. Love for us isn't the same as it is for you. Here, in America, you sing for it as an uncontrollable passion that sweeps the lovers out of their ordinary lives and transforms them, but love for us is more like the music of the sitar: it doesn't rush toward a climax but grows slowly and almost invisibly like a great tree. For us love most often comes after marriage." He smiled ironically. "It's strange I should be saying all this to you because, you see, I love you in the Western way. Yet I am asking you to love me in the Eastern way—to marry me and trust that your heart will follow."

"And if it doesn't?"

"It will, I promise you."

She looked down at the box in her hands, at the ladies sitting beside the pool listening to distant music, and she knew that she had to tell him the ugly, plain, unadorned truth. "I was completely in love once, with someone else—a poet."

Mila's face tightened and he let go of her hand. "Oh," he said, "I didn't know. What was he like, this poet?"

"Unkind, crazy, not very dependable."

"You suffered?"

"Yes, I suffered."

He seized her hand again. "I hate this man who made you suffer; the thought of anyone causing you pain is unbearable to me. I would like to take him and strip him and tie him to a thorn tree and let the wild tigers feast on his intestines."

The thought of David stark naked waiting for the tigers had an undeniable appeal. Lucy smiled despite herself. "Thanks, but that's probably not going to be necessary. The last I heard he was out in San Francisco destroying himself with drugs, and no tiger could do a better job."

"Good," Mila said grimly. "I'm glad to hear that, because you're going to be my wife. I will defend you against all suffering, and any man who causes you the smallest pain in the future will regret it a thousand times over."

She started to protest again, but he wouldn't let her. "I don't care what your past is or how many wicked poets you once loved. I only want you now, in the present, and I warn you, I'm a very determined person who has been terribly spoiled. I'm used to getting what I want, and I want you, Lucy, my dear friend. I'll win that heart of yours."

"I wish that were true." She suddenly felt sad and lost and a bit ridiculous, and she wished—not for the first time—that she had never met David Blake. Taking off the diamonds, she put them back in the box, closed the lid, and sat for a moment looking at the ladies and the swans. How innocent they seemed; how she longed for that kind of peace. "I'm not sure I have a heart left."

"You wonderful woman!" Mila cried, embracing her. "Of course you have a heart! You don't believe me? Then I'll prove it to you." He kissed her hands and her neck and her bare chest. "Here it is, right here. I can feel it beating. I know that heart of yours; I know your goodness and your noble nature. And if you are really convinced that you can't love anyone completely ever again, then I know how to cure that. I know where the love in you is hiding, and I know how to make you feel it."

"Mila, don't; it's just no use."

"You think I'm making wild promises that I can't keep. But you're wrong. I can keep them."

Lucy gave up. It was useless trying to reason with him. She wished he could do everything he promised, but he obviously had no idea what he was up against.